The Red
Rose

The Red Rose

Two pawns. One game. The winner takes the crown.

Victoria Langfeld

THE RED ROSE
TWO PAWNS. ONE GAME. THE WINNER TAKES THE CROWN.

iUniverse books may be ordered through booksellers or by contacting:

iUniverse
1663 Liberty Drive
Bloomington, IN 47403
www.iuniverse.com
844-349-9409

ISBN: 978-1-5320-8946-6 (sc)
ISBN: 978-1-5320-8947-3 (e)

Library of Congress Control Number: 2021912941

Print information available on the last page.

iUniverse rev. date: 06/25/2021

Dedicated to Emily LaRose, my story buddy forever and always. Thank you for believing in me and in this book since it was only scribbles on a page.

Chapter 1

A thick fog had fallen over the forest and I squinted through the blinding rain, attempting to discern where I was. From my perch atop my white stallion, Marquis, I managed to make out the faint outline of the black, iron gates, standing solemnly in front of the stone castle which rose behind it.

A small smile played at the corners of my mouth as I thought about how my parents would react when they saw me, dripping wet and covered with mud. I pictured my father attempting to stifle a laugh, the crinkles around his eyes deepening as my mother paced, lecturing me for being so irresponsible. I could almost hear her now, reminding me that I was supposed to be doing schoolwork, not playing in the woods like a child.

Suddenly, Marquis stopped in his tracks, letting out a high pitched whinny. I gave him a soothing pat, wondering why he seemed nervous. I clicked my tongue and dug my heels into his flanks, trying to get him to keep going. Instead, he bucked and my heart lurched as I clung to his mane, trying to keep my seat in the saddle.

"Marquis, stop," I cried, managing to grab hold of the reins again. I pulled as hard as I could but he fought against the bit in his mouth. Refusing to obey my command, he turned around and began to gallop back into the forest.

My blonde hair whipped wildly in the wind as rain pounded down in torrents around me. A flash of lightning lit the dark sky and the rumble of thunder rang in my ears.

Marquis rose up on his hind legs and this time, my hands grasped at empty air as I tumbled to the ground. I felt a jolt of pain shoot through my body as all the air left my lungs. I laid there, letting the cold, wet earth seep through my clothes while raindrops fell on my face.

My heart slowed its furious racing and my mind reeled with questions. *What had spooked Marquis? He had never bucked before.*

Puzzled, I pushed myself to my feet, letting oxygen flood my burning lungs. My head began to throb and my vision blurred as I scanned my surroundings for any sign of my horse. Knowing he was long gone, I let out a heavy sigh and wiped my mud stained hands on my riding pants. I would have to go back and look for him once the storm was over and the rain had let up.

Disoriented, I stood in the middle of the forest, trying to figure out which direction I had come from. I had ridden Marquis along every trail in these woods since I was a little girl but now, all the trees looked the same.

I took a few steps forward, eyeing the churned up mud beneath my boots. The deep hoof prints were easy to make out in the soft ground and I followed them until I made it back to the trail. My body shook and my teeth rattled together while I walked, hugging my arms tightly to my chest.

After what felt like hours but could only have been a few minutes, I caught sight of the palace, looming in the distance. Relief filled me as I trudged towards my home. A shiver ran down my spine from the cold and I hoped Mother had asked a maid to draw me a hot bath with a cup of chamomile tea.

My heart leapt to my throat and I stopped in my tracks. Blood pounded in my ears, drowning out the sound of the storm around me. Two royal guards laid in a crumpled heap outside the gate. My stomach roiled at the sight of the dark, red stains that covered their blue and white uniforms. My chest tightened as dread gnawed at my insides.

Letting out a shaky breath, I stepped around the bodies and peered through the locked gate. The courtyard was empty and my heartbeat quickened when I realized there were no guards standing near the front entranceway. Unease washed over me while I stood there, listening to the sound of the raindrops pelting against the stone.

A rough hand clamped over my mouth, silencing the scream that rose in my throat. A sharp pain shot through my left shoulder as my arms were wrenched behind my back and securely tied. I winced at the sting of gnarly rope which bit into my skin. With all the strength I could muster, I jerked forward and attempted to spin out of my captor's grasp.

Out of the corner of my eye, I caught a glimpse of a hulking man with a devilish gap-toothed grin before his fist met the side of my head. I cried out as my body slammed against the gate and I fell to the ground, landing partially on top of the bodies which laid in front of it. I gagged, heaving up the contents of my stomach as I tried to get away from the corpses.

The man let out a dark chuckle when I got to my feet, shaking with fear and nausea. Every part of me wanted to run for the forest but I knew I would never make it in my current state.

As if reading my mind, the man said, "I wouldn't go running away if I were you, little lady."

Startled, I looked at him, wondering if he could hear my heart hammering in my chest. Rainwater dripped from his black hair and ran down the sides of his face. His grey eyes met mine and I held his fierce gaze.

The man lunged at me, gripping the neck of my shirt in one hand and pulling me to him. I screamed at the top of my lungs, hoping someone would hear me and come to my aide before this man hurt me.

"Scream all you want, girl, no one will hear you," he said, scooping me up and slinging me over his shoulder like a bale of hay.

I continued to scream and struggle, attempting to escape his iron grip. Questions filled my mind as the gate creaked open and we entered the courtyard. I caught a glimpse of another man lurking behind the palace gate as we passed through and approached the front doors.

My mind raced with endless possibilities, each one worse than the last. *Was this an attack from one of the rebel groups that often rose up in the villages, perhaps discontent with the recent rise in the price of taxes?* They weren't usually this bold, preferring to riot in the town square, break the occasional shop window and then disband.

Or could this be an assasination attempt on my family's life, trying to abolish the Andonine royal family and the monarchy?

My breath caught in my throat as another thought came to mind. *Maybe the neighboring country of Akonia had finally invaded.* I knew Oberia's alliance with them had been thin after Father refused to send soldiers to help fight in their war against Inderlin. But none of these ideas lined up with the situation.

As we neared the entranceway, the large oak doors swung open and a tall man with slick red hair and hawk-like eyes appeared.

"Take her to the dining room," he instructed.

My captor obeyed, taking the hallway on the right, lined with oil paintings of long-dead ancestors, their hollow eyes boring into me as we passed. We entered another hallway and I once again attempted to twist my way out of the man's grasp.

"Put me down," I said, angrily.

"Not a chance," came his gruff reply. He continued on down the hallway, approaching the door to the dining room.

How did he know the way? I thought to myself. I had never seen this man before today. *And where were my parents?* I could only hope they had not been harmed.

The dining room was dark, lit only by a flickering lantern in the center of the long table which stretched nearly the length of the room. Eerie shadows danced up the walls like flames.

The man finally set me down and I wobbled unsteadily on my feet. The ceiling spun and the plush carpet beneath me felt as if it was shaking.

In the darkness, I heard the sound of a chair being pushed out from the table and the muffled sound of footsteps approaching. I could faintly make out the ghostly silhouette of a robed figure.

"Hello, Arianna. I'm pleased you could join us."

My heart skipped a beat at the sound of an unfamiliar man saying my name. His deep, bass voice echoed in the large room, sending shivers down my spine.

"Don't talk to her, Draxon."

My pulse quickened at the sound of my mother speaking.

"Who is Draxon?" I asked with confusion.

"I suppose I haven't been properly introduced to my *niece*. Shame on you, Stephen."

The room flooded with light as a guard lit the large torch which hung on the wall near the head of the table.

A tall man in a black and red robe with dark hair and a speckled handlebar moustache stood beside my parents who were tied to the dining room chairs with thick rope. His skin was pale, his cheekbones high, and his cold eyes were framed by thick, black lashes.

I stood there, stunned. No amount of acting could hide my horror. Draxon had called me his niece, but my father had told me he was an only child.

His cold eyes locked with mine.

"What do you want?" I asked quietly with an edge to my voice.

"I'm glad you asked," replied Draxon with a sly smile. "Have a seat." He gestured to the oak table, proceeding to sit in one of the chairs himself.

My parents exchanged worried glances. "Draxon," my father warned, "leave our daughter out of this."

My heart thudded dully in my chest as the man who had remained at my side during this exchange led me over to the table and pulled out a chair across from Draxon. I sat reluctantly, suddenly reminded of the coarse rope which bit into my wrists. I grimaced and Draxon cast an inquisitive look in my direction. Noticing that my arms were tied behind my back, he gestured to my captor to release me. The man looked warily at me before obeying.

"Clear the room," ordered Draxon with a wave of his hand.

I watched with growing dread as the handful of men that lined the room left, like puppies running away with their tails between their legs after they've been scolded. The door shut with a bang that echoed off the stone walls. Silence hung between us as I looked from Draxon to my parents, unable to deny the look of fear in their eyes.

"As you asked," began Draxon, tapping his long, bony fingers against the tabletop in a repetitive fashion, "what do I want from you?"

I toyed with the button on the collar of my shirt while I waited for his response, trying my best to remain calm and collected.

"All I want is a red rose," Draxon said, pausing to let this sink in. "But not just *any* red rose, but *the*," he emphasized, "Red Rose."

Confusion washed over me and dozens of questions filled my mind. *What was he talking about? Why does he want a red rose? And what does this have to do with me?*

"I don't understand," I said, glancing over at my parents to see their response.

My father's brow furrowed and he looked worriedly at my mother. They exchanged an unreadable glance as they locked eyes with each other.

Draxon leaned back in his chair and crossed his arms over his chest before speaking. "Arianna, do you believe in magic?" he asked, watching me closely.

My heart skipped a beat. *What was he talking about?* "Of course not," I said with a scoff. "I'm not a child anymore."

Draxon chuckled and a faraway look entered his eyes. "I didn't either, but now…." His voice trailed off.

I looked to my parents, wondering if they thought he was as crazy as I did.

"Draxon, stop fooling around and tell us what you really want," said my father, angrily.

"Yes, I'm getting to that," said Draxon with a hint of annoyance in his voice. "You never were very patient, brother."

My father cringed, looking at me apologetically, as if that could fix everything.

"Is he really your brother?" I asked my father, looking between the two with disbelief.

He took a deep breath. "I'm sorry Arianna, I should've told you. But I had my reasons."

I looked at Draxon who was watching us with amusement. His dark features stood in stark contrast to my father's sandy coloured hair and blue eyes. I wondered how they could be brothers and why my father would have kept this a secret from me all these years. More questions swarmed through my head, adding to the growing mountain of secrets and lies.

"Why did you tie my parents up? What does a red rose have to do with all of this?" I asked, still trying to connect the dots.

There was a mysterious glint in Draxon's eye as he began to speak. "I have a proposal for you, my dear," he said.

My chest tightened at the term of endearment and I had a sudden urge to slap the sly smile off Draxon's face.

"I am not your dear," I growled, "or your niece no matter what anyone might say."

Annoyingly, my words only seemed to widen his grin. "Blood is blood, Arianna and unfortunately, we don't get to choose our family."

I remained silent, my hands clenched into fists at my side.

"However," Draxon continued, "blood will mean nothing in a world where I have control over life and death itself. Many claim the Red Rose is simply an ancient Oberian legend but I know it's real."

I felt a growing sense of dread as he spoke. Real or not, no one should possess that kind of power.

"That's where you come in," Draxon said, staring at me with his fierce, dark eyes. I felt as if I was looking into a bottomless pit, the blackness swallowing me whole. "You, Arianna, are the one who will get me the Rose."

A cold, hard laugh escaped me and I looked once more at my parents, as if at any moment they would somehow come untied and tell me this was a joke. But all the light had left their eyes and they shifted uncomfortably against the bristly rope that bound them as they sat there.

"You can't be serious," I said, looking at Draxon with disbelief. "You expect me to get you a magical flower I know nothing about that probably doesn't even exist? And for what? Why should I listen to you?"

"Well," said Draxon, leaning forward in his chair to rest his elbows on the table, "if you don't do exactly as I say—" He stood abruptly, knocking his chair over in the process and calling out to his men who were waiting outside the door.

I watched with horror as five burly guards rushed into the room, their swords drawn. Draxon motioned to my parents who were helpless to defend themselves as the men approached. Two of them held their swords to my parents' necks. They quivered under the pressure of the blade against their skin and I could see the glint of metal in the pupils of their eyes.

My nails dug into the palms of my hands as I squeezed them even tighter, trying to resist the urge not to jump up and tackle Draxon. But I knew his men or whoever they were would be on me in an instant and I was no match for them.

"You wouldn't dare," I spat, but judging by the looks of fear on my parents' faces, his threat was not empty.

"Are you willing to test that theory?" asked Draxon with an arch of his eyebrows.

Seeing my hesitation, his eyes narrowed as he approached me and brought his face close to mine. I sat frozen in my chair, heart racing. I could feel his hot, stale breath on my face but I refused to back away. Suddenly, he reached out and grabbed my neck in his cold hands. I tried to resist, which only made his vise-like grip tighten.

"Now let's see," whispered Draxon in my ear, "you will get me the Red Rose or else…." He gestured to my parents who were huddled together, looking frightened and vulnerable with swords still pressed against their throats. I felt the tension in the room like a rope pulled taut, ready to snap at any moment.

"Don't do it, Arianna," cried my mother.

"Leave her alone," exclaimed my father, angrily.

"So," prodded Draxon, "make your choice." He let go of my neck and I gasped as oxygen once again flooded my lungs.

I looked at my parents and my eyes locked with my mother's. In an instant, I saw a thousand unsaid words flash across her face and I knew, despite all my confusion and uncertainty, that getting this rose was the only way to save my parents.

I looked beside me to see Draxon holding out his hand. I hesitated, looking deep into his eyes, trying to see if he could be trusted. He had the eyes of a liar but what other choice did I have? I couldn't leave my parents at Draxon's mercy. My hand locked with his icy one in a handshake.

"So, do we have a deal then?" asked Draxon, with an evil glint in his eyes.

"Yes," I said. A shiver ran down my spine as I realized I had just sealed my fate with the devil.

Chapter 2

"Why are you doing this?" I asked Draxon as he returned to his seat across from me at the table. He did not offer a response.

"Take them to the dungeon," he ordered the two men who stood by my parents.

Anger bubbled up inside of me at the thought of my mother and father, Oberia's king and queen, locked away in a cold, dirty, rat-infested cell, chained up like animals.

"You won't get away with this, Draxon," said my father with a glare as he was led away.

"I already am, brother," he replied, forcing a cold smile.

The door slammed shut behind them, leaving me alone with a monster.

"Now Arianna, we have things to discuss," Draxon said.

A sick feeling began to form in my stomach as he produced a tattered yellowing cloth from a pocket on the inside of his robe. He placed it on the table between us, attempting to smooth out the wrinkles. It was a map of Oberia surrounded by the Aquarian Sea. The ink was faded but thankfully still legible. Near the bottom of the cloth at the nape of the Raven River was an X which I knew must be where the Red Rose was supposedly located.

"How do you know this magical rose is real and not a made up story? And why do I have to be the one to do this? You have the map, why don't you get it yourself?" I asked Draxon, frustration evident in my voice.

Across the table, Draxon reached for my arm but I jerked it away. "Don't you dare touch me," I said angrily.

"I want to show you something," he said. "Roll up the sleeve on your left arm."

"Why?" I asked him, suspiciously. An uneasy feeling filled me at Draxon's request.

He let out an exasperated sigh. "Please listen to me, Arianna. You're the one who wanted an explanation."

Curiosity got the better of me and I reluctantly rolled up my sleeve as he had asked. The fabric, still wet from the rain, clung to my skin and I probably could have wrung it out.

"There," I said with a shrug, "Now what does this have to do with anything?"

Draxon hesitated for a brief second before he reached across the oak table once more and turned my arm over so the inside was facing up. I grimaced at his touch, fighting the urge to pull away. Confused, I met his gaze, as if it held all the answers I was seeking. His eyes were a dark abyss, a whirlwind of secrets and lies.

His icy finger ran up my arm, tracing a faint red mark on my skin.

"What?" I followed his hand and was able to discern the outline of a rose.

The room spun and suddenly, I wasn't in the dining room sitting at the oak table anymore. I was five again, sitting on the lawn in the garden behind the palace, the grass tickling my toes as I had a tea party with my dolls. My mother was reading a novel while my father sifted through some important looking papers.

Then, *he* appeared. His gaze found mine and he fixed me with a stormy glare which made me tremble with terror.

My mother jumped up from her chair on the lawn nearby, her book which she had been reading falling to the ground with a soft thud. My game forgotten, I immediately ran to her side and stared up into her pale, fear stricken face. I clutched her skirt and hid behind it, poking my head out only at the sound of heavy footsteps approaching.

I don't specifically remember when my father arrived, but he did. He stood protectively at my mother's side, as if saying, "you'll have to go through me first before you'll ever lay so much as a finger on my family."

"Draxon," he said calmly, his voice never wavering for a second. "How did you get in here? I'll call for the guards," he threatened.

"It's nice to see you too, Stephen," he replied coolly.

The tension was like a brick wall between them. I wasn't sure who *Draxon* was, but I wanted him gone. I clutched tighter to my mother's skirt.

"What do you want?" my father questioned firmly. "We presumed you were dead."

There was a pause in the conversation as Draxon pondered his response. He glanced at my father coyly. "You really thought I was dead?" He let out a cold chuckle, laughing at the idea.

"You know what I came for, Stephen. I came for the crown. *My* crown."

My father gritted his teeth. "As long as I'm alive, you'll never get it and even then my daughter will be next in line to wear the crown," said my father, glancing in my direction.

"I'm well aware of that, Stephen," said Draxon, his lips twitching with a smile. "Why do you think you have that scar?" He motioned to the faint red line protruding from underneath my father's collared shirt and running up his neck.

My father instinctively reached up and tugged at his collar as if he could cover the jagged red mark that snaked across his skin.

Fear gripped me as I watched, trying to make sense of the situation. As if suddenly remembering I was there, Draxon turned and began to approach me.

"And who is this little girl?" he asked, a devilish smile tugging at the corners of his mouth. He stooped down to my level and looked into my eyes where I remained at my mother's side.

"Leave my daughter alone," warned my father, his face flushed red with anger.

"She has my eyes," Draxon said with a haunting laugh that rang in the quiet air.

"My daughter has nothing in common with you," spat my father, clenching his hands into fists.

"Come here," the man said in a sickly, sweet voice, reaching out his arms towards me.

Heart racing furiously in my chest, I tried to back away but there was nowhere to go. Draxon scooped me up in his cold arms and held me tight.

"What's your name?" he asked me.

Tears burned the backs of my eyes and I let out a whimper.

"Get your hands off my daughter," exclaimed my father, rushing towards me as my mother began to cry.

"Now, now," Draxon said, pulling away so my father could not take me from him. "I mean no harm," he insisted.

I remained still, unsure what to do. I had no idea who this man was but it was clear my parents were afraid of him.

"What's your name?" he asked me again.

"Arianna," I stammered after a long hesitation. I looked to my father, confused as to what was going on.

"Such a pretty name," Draxon said, shifting my weight to his other arm. As he did, I stretched out my arms towards my father, attempting to squirm my way out of his grasp.

"What is this?" he asked, the smile immediately dropping from his face. My heart skipped a beat as Draxon grabbed my left arm roughly and began to examine it.

The faint reddish pink outline of a rose could be seen on the surface of the skin on my arm.

"I will not say it again," repeated my father with a menacing growl. "Leave my daughter alone."

Victoria Langfeld

Draxon continued to study the mark on my arm with an intense curiosity, muttering under his breath as he did so. His long, gnarled nails trailed over my skin sending shivers up my spine.

"Guards," exclaimed my father, his patience clearly worn thin.

At my father's cry, Draxon set me down on the lawn and began to make his way towards the wrought iron gate at the back of the garden.

"You can't keep me away forever, Stephen," Draxon said with a snarl. "I'll be back one day for my crown and—" He cast a glance in my direction where I stood, shaking on the grass beside my dolls— "The girl."

With a swish of his long black cloak, he opened the gate and ran for the forest which surrounded the palace.

"Arianna," came Draxon's leering voice, pulling me from my memories and back to the present.

I jerked my arm away from Draxon, pulling my sleeve back down. "It's just a birthmark," I said, repeating what my parents had told me many times over the years, every time I asked them about it.

"We've met before," Draxon said, ignoring my explanation. He watched me closely to see my response.

"Yes," was all I could say.

"So you *do* remember?" He said it more as a statement than a question.

"Yes," I said again, "But how—?"

Draxon silenced my question by holding up a hand and pressing one finger to his lips. "Let me explain. When I came back here twelve years ago, my intention was to fight for the crown, but when I saw you...." His voice trailed off as he sat at the table, staring intently across the room, deep in thought.

"I had heard whispers of the Red Rose around the village, a mythical flower possessing magical capabilities. I never believed a word of it until the day I saw that mark on your arm. For years I've searched for any information I could find on it, trying to figure out what the mark meant and how they were connected, if at all," he explained.

"It doesn't mean anything," I insisted, my voice rising as I spoke.

"Do you really believe that?" Draxon asked, his eyes boring into mine.

My heart skipped a beat as I considered everything he had told me. *Could the rose on my arm really be more than a birthmark, something connected to this magical flower Draxon spoke of?*

I shook my head, refusing to believe it. Magic wasn't real, only a figment of childhood imagination inspired by ancient fairytales.

"Over the years, I have traveled all over Oberia in search of the truth about the Red Rose and it has led me back to you," said Draxon.

"What are you talking about?" I said, my voice barely above a whisper. Fear filled me as I sat there, staring at Draxon while he pondered his next words.

"You, Arianna, are the *Keeper* of the Rose, the only one who can retrieve it. Don't ask me how or why because I can't explain it."

My head spun with questions as the realization of what Draxon had said finally hit me. He reached into his cloak and pulled out a small, blue velvet bag and set it gently on the table between us. I looked up into Draxon's dark, hollow eyes, trying to figure out what he was thinking.

I tentatively reached out a hand and pulled the blue velvet bag across the oak table towards me. Draxon made no move to stop me. I picked up the bag and undid the drawstring, peering inside it to see its contents. I pulled out a small, wooden box with a rose engraved on its surface. I felt a slight tremor travel up my spine as I opened it. My breath caught in my throat.

Inside, lay a golden compass with intricate carvings and designs around the edges. There was a dark, blood-red rose in the center of the compass. I traced my finger along the engravings, following the path of a vine that wrapped around it.

"It's beautiful," I whispered.

"Yes, it is," Draxon agreed. "The compass is at least a thousand years old."

"What is it for? How did you find this?" I asked, suspicion creeping into my voice.

"The compass is enchanted," he said in a low voice. "In the hands of the *Keeper,* it will lead you to the Red Rose."

My heart skipped a beat. *Why did Draxon keep insisting I was the Keeper of the Rose?* I didn't know anything about magic or mythical flowers and yet he claimed they were real.

"I'm not the *Keeper,*" I said, my voice wavering. "The mark on my arm doesn't mean anything. You need to wake up and stop living in this fantasy world of yours. Magic isn't real. The Red Rose isn't real," I exclaimed, jumping up from my chair, my voice rising in pitch.

"Arianna," said Draxon with a glower, rising from his seat across the table from me to look me in the eyes. "I don't care if you believe me or not. You will leave tomorrow," he said firmly. "All I am asking of you is to bring me the Red Rose and your parents will live."

Fear coursed through my veins at his words. Gamble or not, I had no choice but to do what he asked. He held all the cards in this game but I would not let him win. The stakes were too high to lose.

I sat on the edge of my bed, still wearing my damp, dirt-stained clothes, staring at the faint outline of a rose on the inside of my arm. So much had happened in only a few hours and my mind could barely process it all. A ghost from the past, an uncle who I hadn't even known existed had returned and was now holding my parents hostage. Our kingdom and the crown was at stake and I was powerless to do anything.

Draxon had given me two choices; to find the Red Rose and bring it back to him or else refuse and surrender my parents' lives and the crown to him. I knew what I had to do.

But doubts crept into my mind nonetheless. I already knew Draxon couldn't be trusted so why should I believe him about this mythical flower? Maybe it was a ploy to get me away from the kingdom so he could kill my parents and take over Oberia.

That didn't explain the mysterious mark on my arm though. Despite my parents' assurances over the years that it was only a birthmark, I had never quite believed them.

My mind wandered to thoughts of my parents and how they must feel, locked away in the dungeon, not able to protect their country or their only daughter who they had done everything to protect.

What if there was a way I could rescue my parents? If we could get safely out of the palace, we could get help to capture Draxon. I couldn't leave them here because the moment he knew I was gone, he would kill my parents without a second thought. And since I wasn't yet eighteen, I had no claim to the throne and the crown would pass to Draxon.

But how could I get from the third floor down to the basement where the dungeon was located? Draxon had likely placed guards in all the halls and on almost every corner.

Adrenaline pulsed through me as I stood up and began to pace my room. There were two men stationed outside my door and it was locked from the outside, making it impossible to escape without causing a commotion. I wracked my brain, trying to come up with a viable solution. I passed my two floor to ceiling bookshelves, running my finger along the worn bindings of my many well-loved books.

Suddenly, an idea came to me. When I was only a young girl of six or seven and had moved into this bedroom, my parents had shown me a number of secret passageways my great grandfather had built into the palace in case of rebel attacks. I knew there was one that ran from my room down to a hidden entranceway in the basement. It would take me almost directly to the dungeon.

Quietly, so as not to alert the men who were standing outside my door, I tiptoed over to the wall in between my dresser and the first bookshelf. I pressed my fingertips into a slight groove in the wall. No one would even notice it was there unless they knew about it.

Slowly the wall slid to the left, creaking and groaning as I pushed on it. When the opening was large enough for me to squeeze through, I stopped to make sure no one had heard. Everything was quiet. I heard the faint jingling of keys as one of the men outside my door shifted positions.

Cautiously, I stepped into the passageway, wary of cobwebs, spiders and small rodents. Reaching for the lantern I knew was always there in case of an emergency, I removed the glass cover protecting the wick. Behind it was a small, half empty paper matchbox.

Opening it, I removed a match and scratched it against the cardboard side. After a number of tries without success, it finally produced a flame. Holding it to the wick once more, it caught fire and was soon burning brightly.

I placed the glass cover overtop and taking one last look at the door to my room, I put the wall back in place, enclosing myself in the tunnel. I needed to hurry so no one would miss me before there was some distance between my family and the palace.

Taking a deep breath, I found the first flight of concrete stairs and proceeded to descend them. The rafters above me were covered in cobwebs which hung down from the ceiling. The small space was filthy and had a musty, unused smell to it. I felt claustrophobic being in such a dark, enclosed area.

I carefully made my way down the spiral steps. A few minutes later, I reached the bottom and found myself face to face with another wall.

I set the lamp down on the last step so it wouldn't get bumped and pushed the wall to the side. Picking up the lamp once more, I entered another passageway, only this time it went two separate ways. One I knew opened up into the second floor and the other continued on further. *But which was which?*

I decided to risk the passage to the right which, as I had suspected, led to another flight of dirty, concrete stairs. I could feel the air getting colder as I neared the basement.

I heard a bang from up above and froze. There was silence and then a voice. After a minute or two, I heard footsteps carry on down the hallway above me and I let out a breath I hadn't known I was holding.

I continued down the last few stairs and then rounded a corner. I found myself smack up against a wrought iron door.

I grabbed the doorknob which felt cool against my sweaty hands. I listened to ensure no one was nearby before pushing with all my might upon the door. It opened with a loud screech as the iron scraped against the concrete.

Sucking in a deep breath, I quickly shut the door, leaving the lantern which I had blown out, before ducking into the shadows.

I heard the sound of pounding boots approaching the door from which I had come. I doubted the men would find it since it blended into the wall. But I was sure they could hear my heart hammering in my chest and even the slightest shift in my uncomfortable position sounded loud amid the quiet.

After a few minutes of looking around without finding anything or anyone out of place, they returned to their posts around the basement. I counted two of them, although there could be more.

Sneaking out from the alcove where I had been hiding, but staying in the shadows, I contemplated my next move.

I could see one of the men stationed at the base of the stairs that led from the floor above. His back was to a door leading outside. I assumed the other one was standing outside the dungeon itself. There was no way I could get past the two of them without getting caught. I could get past the one standing at the base of the stairs as it was a circular strip with a wall in between and I could go around the other side, but the second man was blocking the only other entrance to the dungeon. I would have to create some sort of a diversion that would keep them occupied long enough for me to open my parents cell, get out of the palace and put some distance between us before our disappearance was discovered.

Before I had the chance to think further, a loud bell began to clang from one of the floors up above. I heard excited cries and the thundering of running footsteps overhead. The door to the basement suddenly opened and a head popped in.

"There's a fire in the second floor bedroom that Draxon is occupying. He said to abandon your posts and come upstairs. He needs all available hands to help put out the fire. It's spreading very quickly!" Without another word, the two men left their positions and raced upstairs. Delighted with my good fortune, I waited until I heard the door slam shut before running from the alcove I had been hiding in toward the inner dungeon where I knew my parents must be located.

"Mother! Father!" I cried excitedly. I ran to the iron bars of their cell and peered into the dark interior. "Are you all right?"

"Arianna?" my parents both asked in unison.

"What are you doing down here?" My father was clearly aghast.

"I came down through the secret passageway. I needed to see you and make sure you were okay. I have to get you out of here." They were both tightly chained to the wall and their feet were in stocks. The stress and exhaustion was clearly evident on their faces.

"Arianna," my father began, "it's too dangerous. You shouldn't be down here. The cell is locked and Draxon's men have the key."

I sucked in a deep breath, attempting to slow my racing heart. "There has to be another way," I insisted. "Let me think." I scanned the dungeon, the normally empty cells now filled with servants, guards and other palace staff who had refused to give their allegiance to Draxon. I needed to find something that could be used to open the lock.

"Arianna, please stop and think about this for a minute," began my father. "The risk is too high. Who knows what Draxon would do in his state of mind if he were to find you down here."

"I know," I said, "but I can't just leave you here to die."

"Sweetie," said my mother, her eyes welling up with tears, "you need to leave us and go get help. It's the only way."

My father nodded his head in agreement. "Draxon must be stopped for the sake of our kingdom, for our people," he said.

I stopped my pacing to look in the eyes. "You expect me to leave you here to be killed by Draxon while I go and get help?" I asked, incredulously. "Not only will you both lose your lives, but Oberia will lose its king and queen. You want me to think about our people, think about what would happen then! Draxon would automatically inherit the throne since I'm not eighteen yet. You would be giving him exactly what he wants."

My parents exchanged worried glances.

I crossed the room to another line of cells where an old, rusted pipe was leaning up against the wall. It was heavier than I expected. I carried it over to my parents' cell, wielding it in my right hand and beginning to smash it against the lock.

"Put that down," exclaimed my father in a loud whisper. "Someone will hear you. Draxon's men will be back any minute and you can't be seen down here because that would put all of our lives in jeopardy."

Dejected, I let the pipe fall to the ground with a clang as I slumped down in front of their cell, leaning my aching head against the cold metal bars and letting my eyes flutter closed. "I can't do this," I said, my voice catching in my throat.

"Yes you can," came my mother's firm voice. "The moment you give up, you let Draxon win."

"Trust me Arianna, I've already made that mistake once before," said my father.

"What are you talking about?" I asked, opening my eyes and turning to face my parents in the dim light of the dungeon.

"It's how I got this," he explained, turning his head so I could see the jagged red line that snaked down his neck, disappearing beneath the collar of his shirt.

I could not suppress the gasp that escaped my lips. Memories of that day in the garden when Draxon had returned filled my mind. "What happened?" I asked, not sure if I wanted to hear the answer.

"It was the night before my twenty first birthday," began my father. "Draxon was only nineteen at the time. The next day was my coronation ceremony and he…." His voice trailed off as he relived that moment so many years ago. "My own brother tried to kill me so he could have the crown."

I stared at my father, as a look of horror crossed my face. An image of Draxon with his icy hands gripping the handle of a knife, digging the blade into my father's skin made my stomach churn. I could almost see his eyes glinting with pleasure as red seeped to the surface.

Through clenched teeth I ground out the words "I will kill him."

"I'm so sorry, Arianna," my father apologized, his eyes shining with unshed tears. "We tried to protect you from him but it seems we've failed."

"No," I choked out. "You were only doing what you thought was best. And I will defeat Draxon. I'll play his little game and I'll get his magical flower. But then I will kill him."

"Arianna," my father protested, "You can't."

"I will," I said, anger burning like fire in my veins. "I will not sacrifice your lives for the sake of the kingdom. Our people need you. *I* need you," I said, trying to make them understand.

The sound of heavy footsteps on the stairs leading down to the dungeon and loud voices echoing off the stone alerted me.

"I have to go," I said, my heart resuming its rapid tempo. "I love you," I said, locking eyes with my mother and then my father through the bars of the cell. I desperately wished I could hug them, one last time.

I ran for the door that led into the secret passageway. The wood screeched against the stone floor as I wrenched it open, pulling it shut behind me as Draxon's men entered the dungeon. I leaned my head against the door, heart pounding in my chest. *Safe.*

But I knew this passageway only offered a temporary solace, an illusion of safety and protection. My life, my parents and my country would never truly be safe until Draxon was dead. And I vowed in my heart that I would not stop until his body laid at my feet with his blood on my hands.

Chapter 3

I awoke with a jolt, heart racing, my body wreathed in sweat. An image of Draxon's men dragging the blade of their swords across my parents' necks lingered in my mind. Faint rays of sunlight cascaded through the lacy white curtains hanging across my window, mocking my fear.

I sat up in bed and immediately a piercing, throbbing pain filled my head, causing my vision to blur. My bones burned with a deep, unsettling ache and it felt as if there was a heavy weight pressing down on my chest, making it difficult to breathe.

Today was the day I would leave my kingdom and my parents behind in search of a mythical flower I wasn't even sure existed. But I had no other choice, none I was willing to consider.

My thoughts were suddenly interrupted by the sound of a key turning in the lock. The door was flung open as one of Draxon's men entered my room. His once starched uniform was now rumpled and his eyes were bleary from lack of sleep. I recognized him as the same man who had captured me at the palace gates.

"I've come to escort you downstairs. Draxon is waiting for you," he said, gruffly.

I slid off the bed where I had fallen asleep last night, still in my clothes from the previous day. My hair was matted and my clothes bore grass stains and dried mud from falling off Marquis.

The man extended his arm to me but I brushed past him and into the dimly lit hallway.

"I don't need an escort," I said with a scowl.

I heard his footsteps quicken behind me but he did not try to hold me back. There was nowhere to run anyways.

As we walked along, I couldn't help but wonder who these men were who had given their loyalties to Draxon. I wondered how they knew him and what had caused them to turn their backs on the crown.

"How do you know Draxon?" I asked, bravely. My question was met with silence as I watched his brow furrow in thought.

"You must know that my family is innocent in all this," I said. "Draxon is a corrupt man who only wants power and—"

"Enough," he exclaimed, startling me into silence.

I could sense the slightest feeling of guilt and regret laid just below the surface of this man's heart and likely the others. For whatever the reason, threats or bribery possibly, these men had given their allegiance to Draxon.

We reached the grand staircase which led to the main floor where Draxon awaited us. He stood like a cold, towering statue, watching me approach with a gleam of satisfaction in his black eyes.

"Arianna, I trust you slept well," Draxon said, in his now familiar drawl. "Are you ready to begin your journey?" he asked.

"Do I have a choice?" I replied.

"Arianna, I did not force you to do this. There is still an alternative."

I glared back at him, disgusted by his nonchalance over the whole situation. His brother's life clearly meant nothing to him.

Draxon handed me a small brown knapsack and placed it in my outstretched hands. "There is a canteen of water and some food to tide you over until you can get some provisions," he explained. He paused for a moment to look me directly in the eyes before speaking again.

"Head straight to the harbour," he instructed me. "You will have to cross the Aquarian Sea by ship in order to get to Destin."

Frustration welled up inside of me as I stared into his leering eyes. "How am I supposed to obtain passage on a cargo ship? No one is going to let a girl accompany their crew."

"I'm sure you will find a way," Draxon said.

A menacing look passed over him and his eyes darkened. "Do not even think about crossing me because you know the consequences if you do. Get me the Red Rose and life will go back to the way it was before."

Dread settled on me like a wet blanket. I knew Draxon's threats were not empty but what worried me the most was the nagging feeling that this was all just a ploy to get me out of the way so he could kill my parents and take over Oberia. But there was no way I could know for sure and I could not risk being wrong. I had to trust that Draxon would hold up his end of the bargain.

Taking one last glance around my home, I opened the oak door, straining against the weight, and stepped outside into the courtyard. I squinted in the brightness, contrary to the dark interior of the palace. *I was really doing this.*

I sucked in a deep breath, trying to calm my racing heart and soothe my churning stomach. No matter what the cost, I would save my parents from this monster of a man who supposedly shared our blood. And I would not hesitate to kill him if I ever got the chance.

The sun beat down on me as I walked and I felt a trickle of sweat run down my neck. I swiped a hand across my forehead, brushing a few stray strands of blonde hair out of my eyes. I stopped in the middle of the dusty dirt road, looking down at the mess of wagon ruts and hoof prints ingrained in the ground. I had only been walking for a few hours but it felt as if it had been days. My stomach gnawed with hunger and my throat burned with thirst.

I scanned the fields that lined the road, a few log homes nestled among the trees. I spied a giant oak tree, its sprawling branches drooping over to offer some much needed shade, I left the road and collapsed underneath it. I stretched out my aching legs and laid my head against the cool bark, letting my eyes flutter closed.

There was a pang of guilt in my gut as I thought about my parents who were back at home, their lives hanging in the balance. They needed me. I had a job to do and sitting here, wasting the day away was not going to save them.

I forced my eyes back open and slung my bag off of my shoulders. I pulled out a metal canteen, unscrewed the lid, and held it to my mouth, letting the water trickle down my parched throat. Knowing I needed to save some water for later, I reluctantly lowered the canteen and put the lid back on.

Rummaging around in my bag, I found a hunk of bread wrapped in a red checkered cloth. My stomach let out a grumble and I ravenously bit into it. I had no idea where this journey would take me but I would make it.

I thought back to my visit with my parents in the dungeon. My chest tightened and anger bubbled up inside of me as the image of the jagged red scar across my father's neck appeared in my mind. *How could a man be cruel and cold-hearted enough to take the life of his own brother?*

The allure of power was strong and had clearly corrupted Draxon's heart. There was no doubt in my mind that he would do whatever it took to get the Red Rose, even if it meant murdering his own brother.

But what would Draxon do once he had what he wanted? He was not a man of his word. But there were no other alternatives. Betraying Draxon was not an option with my parents' lives at stake but if I did as he asked, what was stopping him from killing them anyways?

An uneasy feeling washed over me, making my stomach sink. I scrambled to my feet and shoved my half-empty canteen of water, along with the remaining hunk of bread, into my bag. I would not waste anymore time sitting around attempting to figure out

Draxon's next move. It was like trying to play a chess game blind-folded. There was no way to know what your opponent was going to do next or what move to make when your turn came.

As I began to walk along the road once again, I rolled up the sleeves on my cotton shirt, now soaked through with sweat. Eyeing the red mark on my arm in the outline of a rose, my heart skipped a beat. My parents had told me I'd had it from birth, that it meant nothing, but now I wasn't so sure.

Could Draxon have been telling the truth about this marking me as the Keeper of the Rose? I had long since put away my childish fantasies about magic and now I was being told it was in fact, real.

The more likely possibility was that my uncle was actually insane, living in a deranged world of make believe after his failed assasination attempt on my father. *But where did that leave me, with a mysterious mark on my arm and an ancient legend about a rose possessing magical powers?*

A cry of frustration escaped my lips and I stopped in my tracks as two squirrels darted across my path from a clump of trees that lined the side of the road.

When had life gotten so complicated? Only a few days ago I had been a child, going for long rides on Marquis when I should be at home doing schoolwork, yet at the same time wishing I could have more responsibilities within the kingdom. Now, I had the lives of not only my parents but all of Oberia in my hands. I wished Draxon could have chosen someone else to get the Rose for him but I knew that by some cruel twist of fate I had been chosen. This was something I had to do.

My heart burned with fury as my hands instinctively balled into fists at my side. A small fire of hatred had been ignited inside of me, the flame slowly growing until it could not be contained. Whether Draxon or some higher power had chosen me, neither could determine my fate. I would play this little game and get the Rose but when this was all over, I would kill Draxon myself for what he had done to my family and my country. No one played with fire without getting burned.

When I arrived at the wharf, the sun was a fiery orange ball on the horizon. Instantly, my nose crinkled at the rank odour of fish which hung thick in the air.

The harbour swarmed with burly, young men carrying large wooden crates and loading them onto the ships. Their white sails blew in the slight breeze and the waves crashed onto the shore, sending foamy spray into the air.

I stood there, gazing at the pandemonium around me and attempted to figure out what I should do next. I needed to find a way to get on one of the cargo ships but I was skeptical that any captain would take me. I scanned the port which contained about a dozen, identical looking ships. I supposed I could just pick one and start there.

A horse-drawn wagon raced past me, the driver spitting over the side and cursing as unsuspecting people darted out of his path. Startled, I jumped out of the way, knocking into a small group of men who were leaning against a pile of lumber drinking beer.

"Watch where you're going, girl," growled one man, taking a swig out of his bottle and wiping a grimy hand across his dirt streaked face.

"I'm sorry," I said, backing away from them.

Before I could walk away, I felt a light tug on my backpack and I whirled around in time to see a young boy with a thick mop of curly brown hair pushing his way through the crowd, trying to make himself disappear. My heart leapt to my throat as my eyes narrowed in on the blue velvet bag containing the compass Draxon had given me that was clutched in his hand.

A wave of panic washed over me. *I needed that compass.*

I began to race after him, keeping my eyes locked on the back of his head bobbing through the crowd. *I couldn't lose him. I couldn't.*

My lungs burned as I forced myself to run faster as the thief neared the docks.

He would not get away with this, I vowed angrily.

Blood pounded furiously in my ears as I raced towards him, quickly gaining ground. Not caring who was watching but knowing that my mother would be appalled at my behaviour, I leapt towards the boy, grabbing hold of his shoulders and wrapping my arms around his neck in a chokehold. We both fell to the ground in front of the docks in a squirming heap of thrashing legs and jabbing elbows.

Using all the force I could muster, I managed to press my shaking hands against the boy's chest, holding him against the ground so he couldn't get up. Stunned, he looked up at me with wide, hazel eyes and I could feel his heart pounding beneath me as he stopped struggling.

"You're pretty fast for a *girl*," he said with a sheepish grin.

"What?" I asked, the torrent of angry words that had risen in my mouth quickly dying, like water thrown on flames.

"I said, you run pretty fast for a girl," he repeated, his smile only widening. I did not miss the mischievous twinkle in his eyes.

My eyes narrowed and I felt my heart skip a beat, unsure what to make of this boy. I took my hands off his chest, snatching the velvet bag out of his grasp, surprised when he did not resist. I stood up, dusting myself off and he stood too, making no move to run away.

I wanted to say something, to yell at him for what he had done but the words caught in my throat as I stood there, watching him smile dumbly back at me. Instead of turning to leave, he reached out a hand and took mine in his, giving it a firm shake.

"I'm Gabriel," he said. "And you are....?" he asked, his brow arching in my direction.

I stammered, caught off guard yet again. *Why did he tell me his name? And why did he care about knowing mine?* Reluctant to use my full name in case he somehow made the connection to my royal background, I hesitated.

"I'm Ari," I said, after a brief pause.

"Well Ari," said Gabriel, flashing me another wide grin, "It's nice to meet you."

Confused and irritated by his manner, I ignored him, slinging my backpack off my shoulders and placing the compass Draxon had given me back inside. Gabriel didn't seem to be aware of the bag's contents or else he likely wouldn't have been so willing to return it. The compass was probably worth a small fortune since it was made from pure gold, not to mention it's connection to the Red Rose.

Picking my bag up again, I started to walk away, but Gabriel began to follow, placing a hand on my arm. I whirled around, heaving a heavy sigh of frustration. "What do you want now?" I asked.

"Where are you going?" Gabriel asked curiously.

"None of your business," I said angrily. "Why would I tell you after you just robbed me?"

He didn't seem offended by my outburst but had the gall to smirk.

"Just wondering," he said, "because if you're heading to the harbour, it's that way," he said, gesturing behind him.

"Oh," I said, my face quickly heating with embarrassment. I pushed past Gabriel and began walking back towards the docks.

"Do you know where I can find a ship headed to Destin?" I asked a man with strawberry coloured hair who was walking by carrying a pile of lumber. He nodded to the ship directly in front of us, its white sails billowing proudly in the warm summer wind.

"The *Maryanne*, that's Cap'n Carter's ship," he answered, eyeing me curiously. "Finest ship on these waters."

"Thanks," I said, not offering any further explanation.

I followed the man up the gangplank of the ship, ignoring the footsteps that followed behind me.

A middle-aged man who was dressed in white pants, a navy blue jacket and a sailors hat with a large black belt around his plump middle stood in the doorway. He stepped to the side to let the man pass with his lumber to be delivered, his gentle green eyes falling on me.

"What can I do for a young lass like you?" he asked.

"I would like to obtain passage on your ship to Destin," I said quickly.

The captain's brow furrowed and he motioned for me to come onto the ship. I had no idea who this man was but I could only hope he would allow me to accompany him.

His office was a small room off to the side of the main deck where a handful of young men dressed in white collared shirts and brown khaki pants swarmed the deck, raising the sails and loading the last of the lumber onto the ship. A large desk littered with papers and nautical charts took up most of the room.

Captain Carter made his way over to the desk where he sat in a hard backed chair behind it, motioning for me to sit on a small stool across from him. I remained standing, looking over my shoulder where Gabriel hovered with that same stupid grin on his face he had when I tackled him.

"What are you doing here Gabriel?" I asked with frustration. "I told you to leave me alone."

"It didn't seem to me like you knew where you were going so I thought I could help. It wouldn't have been right for me to leave a pretty young woman all alone," he said.

I glared at him. "Well I'm here now and perfectly capable of looking out for myself so you can leave now."

"That's all the thanks I get?" Gabriel asked with an arch of his brows. I could see the twinkle in his eyes and I curled my hands into fists at my side at his arrogance.

"I never asked for your help," I said through clenched teeth.

"I'm sorry, is there a problem here?" asked Captain Carter with concern, looking back and forth between the two of us.

Gabriel looked at me, as if daring me to tattle on him. I stared right back and our eyes locked, each of us challenging the other to back down first. After a tense moment of silence, Gabriel shook his head with a chuckle.

"I'll be waiting outside," he said, sauntering towards the door. He gave me one last look over his shoulder before shutting the door behind him.

I let out a groan as I sat down on the stool across from Captain Carter.

"What's going on?" he asked, studying me intently.

I ducked my head, fiddling with a loose string on my pants, trying to figure out what to say.

"I have to get something in Destin," I said, vaguely. "I was hoping I could obtain passage on your ship but I don't have any money to pay you."

I had only brought a few gold coins with me, tucked away in my backpack. I didn't want to bring lots of money with me because that would make me an easy target for bandits and pickpockets and would draw too much attention to myself.

Captain Carter's lips turned up with surprise at my request. "What business does a young lass like you have in Destin?"

"It's a complicated story," I said, letting out a deep sigh.

"I won't ask questions," he replied, raising his brows in my direction. "You may have passage on my ship if you like. In exchange, how would you feel about doing some cooking and cleaning to help out?"

"I will do anything," I said, surprised the Captain had granted my request. "Thank you so much."

"Who is that boy that came here with you?" asked Captain Carter, changing the subject and leaning back in his chair.

I felt my face flush and I stammered to find the words to say. "I met him today at the wharf and now he won't stop following me," I explained with exasperation.

"He seems like a nice boy," he said, watching my face closely to see my reaction.

He was a nice boy, besides the fact that he tried to rob me, I thought to myself. I wasn't sure why I hadn't told Captain Carter that part. There was no reason for me to protect him or uphold his reputation. Gabriel was clearly a boy on the streets trying to survive the only way he knew how but that didn't mean his actions should go unpunished.

Captain Carter furrowed his brow in thought. "I know you just met him but do you trust him?"

No. His lopsided grin, that mischievous twinkle in his eyes and his infuriating arrogance made me feel uneasy. That boy was trouble.

"I don't know," I said. "Why do you want to know?"

"I was thinking the boy might like a job on the *Maryanne*. I could use another young man to help with chores and unloading all the lumber when we get to Destin."

My stomach sank as he spoke. There was no way I could put up with Gabriel on the ship for a whole week.

"I won't ask him if you aren't comfortable with the idea," added Captain Carter.

I shifted uncomfortably on the stool. "You can ask him, I guess," I said with a shrug. "I doubt he would be interested though."

He stood with a smile and made his way over to the door. "Gabriel," he called out. "Could you come here for a minute?"

I suppressed a groan as Gabriel entered, his curly brown hair tousled by the wind. He rested one hand in the back pocket of his tattered black pants.

Captain Carter shut the door behind him and walked back over to stand behind his desk. "Would you consider joining the crew on this ship for our voyage to Destin? I could use an extra hand to help with chores and unloading lumber," he explained.

Gabriel's eyes immediately lit up with a twinkle as he looked at me. I rolled my eyes in annoyance.

"I would love to," he replied. "Thank you so much Captain Carter." He approached the desk and held out a hand.

Captain Carter took it with a smile. "We'll be departing shortly so you can go give the other men a hand on deck," he said.

"Of course." He cast a grin my way as he headed for the door. "See you around, Ari."

My heart skipped a beat. "See you," I said, forcing a smile of my own. *Yes*, I thought to myself, *Gabriel was definitely trouble.*

Chapter 4

I stood on the deck of the ship as the warm wind blew my blonde hair into my face. I didn't bother to brush it away. The ship rocked gently beneath my feet as it began to pull away from the dock.

The white sails rustled in the breeze as the sailors worked to fasten it to the mast. The waves became larger as we moved farther away from land and I felt my heart race a little faster.

This was it. I felt like I was abandoning my parents but I knew this was what I had to do in order to save them.

I looked over my shoulder to see a group of young men gathered in a small circle on the deck, their raucous laughter ringing in the open air. My eyes fell on Gabriel who stood with them, the sun falling across his tanned, dirt streaked face. His eyes twinkled with laughter as he listened to the conversation of the other young men.

As if feeling my gaze on him, he looked up and our eyes met. I felt heat rising up my neck and into my cheeks, causing me to look away. Not wanting to be near him in case he decided to come over and talk to me, I walked briskly in the opposite direction. Maybe Gabriel could win the trust and friendship of the sailors but I would not fall for his charm. I could not take the risk of trusting anyone right now.

Rounding the corner to another part of the upper deck, I saw a set of stairs leading down into the belly of the ship. Curious, I decided to see what was down below. As I began to descend the creaking staircase, I blinked a few times to help my eyes adjust as the sun from above slowly faded. There were a few portholes where faint rays of sunlight cascaded through.

There was a large open area off to the right filled with lumber and rows of crates stacked to the ceiling with supplies. They would be delivered to Destin, a mill town, where the rest of the country got most of their flour, sugar and oatmeal from. Trading ships went there often from Aurora, the capital city, to deliver lumber, stone, nails and other essential tools.

I peered in a doorway on the left to see rows of bunk beds, enough to sleep eight people. I would have to speak with Captain Carter about my sleeping arrangements because there was no way I was going to sleep in the same room as the rest of the sailors.

Taking one last look around, I left the ship's sleeping quarters and entered the last room straight ahead of me. There was a long counter with a small wood stove beside it. A table sat in the center of the room with four hard-backed chairs. There was a wash basin in the corner and a few empty barrels had been turned upside down to provide extra seating.

I absently wandered over to a cupboard above the counter and opened it. A small stack of tin plates and cups lined the shelf and there was some silverware thrown in with them. I chuckled as I opened the next cupboard. There was a small bag of flour and an empty pitcher inside. I wondered what these men ate on their long voyages. *How had they not starved to death?* I doubted any of them knew how to cook.

Growing up, we had a chef and other kitchen staff who prepared all our meals for us but despite this, my mother had still insisted that I learn. She had grown up on a big family farm and had always helped her own mother make meals. Maybe my cooking skills would finally be put to good use.

I heard heavy footsteps descending the stairs and I let the cupboard door slam shut with a bang. Captain Carter appeared in the doorway to the kitchen, resting his arm on the door frame.

"Ari, I wondered where you had disappeared too," he said with a chuckle. "I see you've been exploring."

"Yes," I said, returning his smile. "I didn't mean to wander off but I've never been on a ship before and I wanted to see what was down here."

"No worries," he said. "The sailors are finishing securing the sails and making sure everything is in order."

"Is there anything I can do to help?" I asked. "It doesn't look like you have much in the way of food and I was thinking that I could help with the cooking."

"There are some more supplies in that barrel over there," explained Captain Carter, gesturing to the far corner. "I don't like to keep food in the cupboards because the rats will get into it," he explained.

I moved towards the barrel he had pointed to and pulled off the lid. There were a few loaves of bread wrapped in brown paper, some cornmeal, a few onions, salt pork and a small bag of apples.

"Normally we eat a lot of biscuits and gravy," Captain Carter said. "It's hard to keep fresh fruits and vegetables when you are at sea for weeks at a time."

"I'll see what I can do," I said.

"And for your sleeping arrangements," continued Captain Carter, straightening his posture against the door frame, "I am getting Gabriel to set up a cot for you in the storage room beside my quarters."

"I appreciate it," I said.

"I hope you will be able to put up with us rowdy men," he said with a twinkle in his eyes. Growing serious he said, "if any of my men are being disrespectful or harassing you in any way, promise me you will come to me right away and they will be dealt with. I will not tolerate that kind of behaviour on my ship."

"Of course," I said immediately, my stomach doing a strange flip-flop. Gabriel's face crossed my mind but I quickly brushed the image away. I was safe on this ship and Captain Carter would not let anyone mistreat me.

He turned to go, his bulky figure disappearing through the door. I let out a huge breath I hadn't even known I was holding. I could handle Gabriel's arrogance and the taunting laughs and jeers of the other men if needed. I was here because I had a duty to my family and to Oberia and no one was going to stand in the way of what I had come to do.

I slung my backpack off of my aching shoulders and set it in the corner of the room. I began to pull supplies out of the barrel as I thought of what I should cook. I had no idea what time it was but the sun had begun to set, causing a red and orange glow to shine through the portholes. It was likely close to seven o'clock and my stomach had begun to rumble with hunger.

I pulled a large stoneware frying pan from a cupboard beside the wood stove, deciding that I would cook salt pork to go with the biscuits that had been wrapped up in the barrel.

While I worked, my thoughts wandered into the past. My father had told me down in the dungeon that Draxon had tried to kill him because he wanted the throne. He had failed once before but there was no one around to stop him from murdering my father now. My eyes blurred with tears and my heart began to race as I wondered if my parents were even alive right now.

I let the knife I was using to cut the pork fall to the floor with a dull clang. I slumped down beside the stove and leaned my head against the cupboards, tears falling down my cheeks.

"I should have stayed, I should have rescued my parents," I cried out angrily, choking on my sobs. "I should have killed Draxon."

A tremor ran through my body as I cried, unable to hold in the tears any longer. I had been protected and shielded my entire life from the hardships of our country. My parents never talked to me about the rebel attacks, the village raids or our crumbling alliance with Akonia. They never even told me about my own uncle because they thought it would be best.

But in the span of only a few hours, I had gone from being a carefree girl with no worries or responsibilities to a woman who had a duty to protect her kingdom. I didn't know how to be that woman and I didn't want to be her. I desperately wished life could go back to normal, to the way things were before.

"Is everything alright?" came a concerned voice, jolting me out of my thoughts.

I leapt to my feet, turning my back to the doorway to face the stove and brushing furiously at my tear-streaked face.

"What are you doing here, Gabriel?" I demanded as I stirred the gravy that bubbled in a pot on the stove. I could feel the heat emanating from inside as the wood slowly burned to ashes.

Gabriel didn't answer but I could hear his footsteps approaching me from behind. I recoiled when I felt his gentle hand on my shoulder.

"Don't touch me," I spat angrily, whirling around to face him. "I don't know who you are or what your motives are but I won't tell you again to leave me alone."

Gabriel lowered his gaze to the floor and took a step back. "I'm sorry Ari. I'm not trying to hurt or upset you. I just wanted to make sure you were okay."

"I'm fine," I said bitterly.

"You don't look fine," Gabriel said. "Actually, you look terrible," he chuckled, the twinkle returning to his eyes.

A small smile tugged at the corner of my mouth as I swiped a hand across my face again.

"Captain Carter asked me to set up a cot for you in one of the storage rooms so why don't you go on up and get settled in."

"I can't," I protested. "What about dinner?" I gestured to the stove where the salt pork was sizzling in the frying pan.

"I know a thing or two about cooking," he said with a boyish grin.

"Really?" I said, unable to hide my surprise.

Gabriel tilted his head back and let out a loud laugh that rang in the quiet room. "I'm offended," he said, holding a dramatic hand to his heart.

"Whatever you say," I replied, walking over to the corner of the room to retrieve my bag.

"Ari," said Gabriel, suddenly falling serious as I turned to leave the kitchen.

"Yes?" I asked, looking back at him curiously.

He brushed away a small brown curl that had fallen into his eyes. "I never apologized for stealing from you. I'm sorry about that. I know we got off to a rough start."

My heart skipped a beat as I looked into his hazel eyes. My impression of Gabriel so far was that he was rarely serious. But I could tell his apology was sincere.

"Apology accepted," I said softly.

There was a short pause as we looked at each other, not sure what to say next. I began to walk towards the door but stopped to look over my shoulder. Gabriel was still standing in front of the stove, watching me.

"I hope you weren't expecting me to apologize for tackling you earlier. You deserved it," I said with a teasing smile.

I heard him protest as I left the kitchen and headed towards the stairs that led to the upper deck.

"I take back my apology," he called out.

I bit my lip, trying to hold back the laughter that bubbled up inside of me.

I reached the top of the stairs to see Captain Carter walking along the deck towards his quarters.

"Captain Carter," I called out, running along the deck to catch up with him.

He stopped in his tracks and turned around at the sound of his name.

"Sorry to bother you," I said, "but Gabriel told me he set up a cot for me as you asked. Do you think you could show me where it is so I can get settled in?"

"Of course," he said with a kind smile, continuing to walk along the deck. "I feel bad that it isn't very spacious or comfortable."

"I don't mind at all," I reassured him. "You have already done so much for me and I am very grateful for your kindness."

He brushed away my words with a wave of his hand. "I haven't done much," he said.

We stopped outside a door directly beside the Captain's office and his adjoining quarters.

"Here we are," he said, opening the door and motioning for me to go in.

I stepped inside the small room which had shelves that ran from floor to ceiling and were filled with crates, rope and some fishing nets. There was a cot on the remaining floor space with two wool blankets and a pillow.

I gave my thanks to the captain and he left me to get settled, shutting the door behind him.

I immediately took off my backpack and flopped down on the cot with a sigh. A lot had changed in a short period of time and it was hard to process everything. I dug through my bag and pulled out the map and the blue velvet bag that held the compass.

I spread out the tattered cloth on the floor in front of me, trying to smooth some of the wrinkles. The ship would take me to Destin but after that it was still a long way to get to where the Red Rose was located at the edge of Raven River.

I wondered how long Draxon would give me before he assumed me to be dead and not coming back. I would have to ask Captain Carter when the next ship would be coming to Destin because that was my only way back to Aurora and I couldn't miss it. If I did, I would have to wait a whole week or more before another ship would be arriving.

Folding the map back up and placing it in my backpack, I pulled the compass out of the velvet bag and held it in my hands. It was heavy and the gold felt cold against my skin. I gently tapped the glass and watched the arrow move back and forth. Draxon told me the compass was enchanted and it would lead me to the Red Rose but I wasn't so sure. *How could a compass direct you to a mythical flower?*

I heard the heavy thumping of boots on the stairs near my room as the sailors descended them, likely heading to the kitchen for dinner. I quickly cupped the compass between my hands as if afraid someone would see it, despite being alone in the cabin.

I was still surprised by Gabriel's kindness towards me and the fact that he knew how to cook. Growing up, I had always been told the kitchen was meant for women and I appreciated a man who wasn't embarrassed or ashamed to help out.

I stood up in the small space between my cot and the door, cringing as a clump of dried mud fell off my pants onto the floor. I knew I looked awful and Gabriel had happily confirmed that fact.

I opened my door and stepped out, shutting it behind me so none of the sailors would go looking through my things. I began to brush at my clothes, attempting to get some of the dried mud and dust that had accumulated over the past two days since I hadn't had the opportunity to change. I wished I had thought to pack an extra outfit or change before I left but my appearance had been the last thing on my mind.

Knowing there wasn't much more I could do to my outfit, I quickly ran my fingers through my hair, trying to get out some of the tangles caused by the wind. After dinner I would have to fill a basin with water and try to clean up a bit more.

Hearing the loud, rambunctious chatter and laughter filtering up from the kitchen below, I headed downstairs to get some dinner. I could smell the aroma of the salt pork and gravy that had been cooking on the stove and my stomach let out a protesting grumble.

"Ari," said Gabriel with a grin as I entered the crowded room. He stood at the stove, filling a plate for himself.

Captain Carter and the other sailors had already gotten their food and were seated at the table or on barrels around the room, eating their meal.

"Here, take this," he said, handing me his plate and grabbing another one from the cupboard above.

"Thanks," I said, with a smile.

Gabriel finished filling a plate for himself and then gestured for me to follow him. "Let's sit over here," he said, leading me towards two barrels that sat against the wall on the far side of the room.

I eyed the other sailors who sat at the table, grateful that I didn't have to try to be friendly and socialize with them right now.

I sat on one of the barrels and leaned my back against the wall, trying to balance my plate and silverware without dropping anything. Picking up my fork and knife, I cut up a small piece of salt pork and brought it to my mouth. Out of the corner of my eye, I noticed Gabriel watching me chew with a smirk on his face.

"How does it taste?" he asked.

"Surprisingly, pretty good," I said, after I had finished swallowing. "A lot better than I was expecting."

"My resources are limited here, remember," he said with a chuckle. "You get me in a real kitchen though and I will fix you a meal fit for a queen."

I laughed but my heart began to race inside my chest. No one here knew who I was but I worried about what would happen if anyone found out. People were bound to start asking questions eventually and I had never thought myself to be a good liar.

My mother used to tell me that my eyes were what gave it away. She always knew if I had snuck a cookie before dinner or had been outside playing instead of doing my schoolwork.

"How did you learn to cook?" I asked Gabriel, curious about this mysterious boy.

He looked away from me and down at his plate, taking a bite of his biscuit before replying.

"My mama taught me," he said. "She never had a daughter so she figured I should learn." His voice grew quiet as he spoke and I could tell there was more to the story than what he was letting on. Everyone had a past but I could tell Gabriel wasn't ready to let anyone else into his.

He seemed like a completely different person than the one who had tried to rob me at the wharf. But that's how people got away with things. The best liars were always the charmers, the sweet ones nobody would suspect.

I hoped Gabriel would turn out to be different.

"So what brings you onto this ship, Ari?" asked Gabriel, looking up at me again.

I shifted uncomfortably on the barrel, not sure what I should say. I didn't want to lie but the truth was definitely not an option. He would probably think I was insane anyways.

"There's something I need to get in Destin," I said. Not exactly a lie but close enough to the truth that I didn't have to feel too guilty.

Gabriel's hazel eyes narrowed slightly and he held my gaze for what felt like an eternity before turning back to his food. Obviously he knew I was holding back information. But games were meant for two.

I picked at the rest of my pork, suddenly losing my appetite. "I'm pretty tired," I said, standing abruptly, "so I think I'm going to head to bed now."

"But it's not even seven o'clock," protested Gabriel, eyeing the large wooden clock mounted on the wall by the door.

"It's been a long day," I said.

Only that morning, I had been at the palace and now I was in the middle of the Aquarian Sea on a ship with a bunch of strange men. I walked away from Gabriel, eyeing the sailors who had set their plates aside to make room for a game of cards.

I set my plate on the counter and slipped out of the room. Someone else could manage the cleanup.

When I reached the top of the stairs, I sucked in a deep breath of salty sea air. Walking over to lean against the railing, I looked out over the water, feeling the gentle sway of the ship as the waves lapped against the sides. The sun was low on the horizon and it looked like a chunk of molten lava melting into the ocean. The sky had turned a dusty grey with streaks of red running across it's never ending canvas. There was nothing for miles but a vast expanse of sea and sky.

An overwhelming feeling washed over me as I stood there. I felt the weight of this great responsibility to my parents and my people that had been thrust upon me.

I placed my hand on my chest and felt the gentle rhythm of my heart beating in my chest. One, two, three. Over and over, beat after beat.

I was only one girl of thousands in Oberia and yet I had the power to decide their fates. Whether they would live or die or be enslaved to an evil king who only wanted the title and the wealth that went with it.

Draxon was only one enemy among many who threatened the lives of my people. There were rebels and power-hungry kings who wanted Oberia for themselves.

It was like a game, fighting for who would be on top, who would be left standing when it was all over. No one would expect a little girl to win against the devil.

I had been called many things in my life. *Angel, princess, darling.*

But *weak* was not one of them. I was not the girl who Draxon thought I was. Even though all the odds appeared to be against me, losing had never been something I did.

I wasn't about to start now.

Chapter 5

I tossed and turned on the small cot, unable to get comfortable. I kicked my blankets to the side and rolled onto my back, staring up at the ceiling. It was unbearably hot in the tiny room and I couldn't sleep no matter how hard I tried.

My mind whirled with thoughts of my parents which consumed me every waking minute. They had always been the ones who had protected me and now it was my turn to protect them. I couldn't let them down.

A sliver of moonlight crept through the crack beneath the door. Unable to stay still, I got to my feet and opened the door, tiptoeing out onto the deck. The wood felt cool against my bare feet and a soft breeze tugged at the bottom of the oversized white shirt I wore that Captain Carter had given to me.

Bright moonlight bathed the ship and my breath caught in my throat as I looked up at the sky where thousands of stars glinted like shards of broken glass.

I walked along the deck, letting my fingers trail against the railing as I looked out at the Aquarian Sea. I had never seen the ocean up close before, let alone been on a ship. The gentle rocking beneath my feet gave me a feeling of peace.

Suddenly, I heard the deep, gentle voice of a boy singing that echoed in the silence. Tugging my shirt down a little farther, I ventured along the deck, following the sound of the haunting melody. I rounded the corner and stopped in my tracks, looking around for the source. There was no one in sight. The voice sounded closer than before and I looked above me to see a small lookout high above, attached to the mast of the ship. There was a railing that wrapped around it but I still didn't see anyone.

I took a few steps closer, spying a tall, rickety ladder that led up to it. Curious, I began to climb it, wondering if the person who was singing was up there. My heart skipped a beat as I made out the shadowy silhouette of a boy sitting on the platform, leaning his back against the railing with his legs stretched out in front of him.

The ladder wobbled unsteadily beneath me and I let out a sharp squeal. I clutched tightly to the rungs of the ladder as my heart pounded in my chest.

The boy had stopped singing and approached the ladder, peering over the edge. His gaze landed on me, standing there shaking in my oversized t-shirt.

"What in the world?" he asked, shaking his head with a grin. "Come on, only a few more steps," he said.

"Is this safe?" I asked, despising the tremor I heard in my voice.

"Perfectly," he said. I saw the twinkle in his eye, not sure whether to believe him or not.

I let go of the rung I had been clinging to with one hand, taking a cautious step upwards.

"Here," said the boy, holding out a callused hand to me. I gratefully accepted it, letting him help me up the last two rungs to the platform.

"Sorry," I apologized, feeling the heat creeping into my cheeks as I stood on the small platform beside him.

"No, it's okay," he said, smirking as he eyed my outfit. "I guess you're Ari," he said.

"So you've heard about me," I said, casting him a teasing smile. "I don't know if I should be flattered or run in the other direction."

"Well, you are the only woman on the ship," he said, "so you do stand out a bit."

"I guess the men's shirt didn't help," I said, laughing. The darkness hid the flush creeping into my cheeks and I could sense he was embarrassed too.

"I'm Darian," he said, holding out his hand to me again.

I accepted the handshake, feeling the strength in his grip. After a long moment, Darian pulled his hand away, and tucked it into the pocket of his khaki pants. His white shirt hung open, blowing in the night breeze.

"So what are you doing up in the middle of the night?" asked Darian.

"I couldn't sleep," I said. "I thought the fresh air might help." The moon shifted in the sky above, illuminating Darian's face. His unruly blonde hair stuck up in the back of his head and his green eyes glinted in the light.

"It's so peaceful at night," he said. "I actually enjoy taking the night shift."

"Night shift?" I asked, curiously.

"The crew members each take turns on lookout," he said, gesturing to a large telescope on the edge of the railing, pointing out to sea.

"It's not usually very exciting," Darian said. "I keep an eye on the weather and make sure the ship stays on course. If there's a problem, I'll deal with it or get Captain Carter."

I nodded. "How do you stay awake?"

"I do a lot of thinking." He let his voice trail off. "Sometimes I sing to myself."

"I heard you singing," I admitted. "I wanted to see who it was."

"Well, you found me," said Darian with an embarrassed laugh, reaching an arm up to run his hand through his tousled hair.

I let out a breath of air, surveying the view before me. The deck below was cast in shadows from the moon and the ocean spread all around us, never-ending.

"Do you want some company?" I asked, my mouth suddenly growing dry. The look of surprise on his face made my heart skip a beat. "Only if you want, I mean, you probably like the time alone—"

"No, company is good," he interrupted, flashing me a grin.

He sat down on the floor, leaning back against the railing. He patted the spot next to him. I sat down, pulling my knees up to my chest.

A gentle breeze ruffled the sails above us as we sat in silence.

"How long have you worked on the *Maryanne* for?" I asked, curiously.

"I've worked on this ship for the past two years, ever since I was sixteen," he said, gazing off into the distance at the horizon.

"What about your family?" I asked hesitantly, not sure how much he was willing to share with me.

He fingered the frayed string that hung on his wrist, toying with what looked like a tiny violin pendant. "I needed to get out on my own and see the world for myself. I felt smothered, like I was seeing the world through their eyes instead of experiencing it for myself." Darian gave me a sidelong glance.

"I don't know if that makes any sense," he said, with a half-hearted smile.

"It does," I said, thinking back on my own childhood. My parents loved me, I had no doubt of that.

Every night my mother would kneel beside my bed and sing an old lullaby her mother had sung to her. My father would always let me have a cookie before dinner and would play hide and seek with me in the woods, even though I knew there were mounds of unopened letters and important papers on his desk to attend to. I had grown up with everything a little girl could ever dream of. But I rarely left the palace grounds. My world ended at the towering iron gate of the courtyard.

I had been sheltered by the stone walls, the barred windows and the guards who always stood watch outside my door at night. The only time I was truly alone was when I would ride Marquis along the trails of the forest which surrounded the palace. Father had not allowed me to ride unaccompanied until I was fourteen after pleading and coaxing him every day until he got tired of my tears and complaints and finally gave in.

"This is the first time I've left Aurora," I said, turning to Darian. "I know what it's like to feel smothered and want to see the world for yourself."

"What made you decide to obtain passage on a cargo ship with a bunch of rowdy men?" asked Darian.

I hesitated, not sure how much I should tell him. I didn't want to lie but the truth wasn't exactly an option.

"There's something I need to pick up in Destin," I explained, repeating what I had told Gabriel earlier. I diverted my gaze to the small, yellow stain in the bottom corner of my t-shirt but I could feel his eyes focused on me.

Thankfully, he didn't press the matter further. I looked up and my eyes met his as the moonlight cascaded across him, illuminating his face in the velvety darkness of the night.

I touched his wrist, fingering the bracelet I had noticed earlier. "Did someone give this to you?" I asked.

"My mother," he replied, his voice growing husky.

I watched his throat bob as he swallowed around the lump that had formed.

It was obvious his mother held a special place in his heart and the bracelet meant a lot to him. I didn't press further out of fear of opening old wounds. Some scars never faded but remained as fresh as the day they were inflicted.

My father had never gotten over his brother's betrayal all those years ago and I knew the memory of that knife held against his throat with Draxon leaning over him would haunt him forever.

"Your parents must miss you," said Darian, resting his arms on top of his knees.

I felt a dull ache in my chest at the thought of my mother and father. I had tried not to think about them, focusing instead on the journey ahead of me and what I had to do to save them. I couldn't afford to let my emotions get the best of me. And I couldn't afford to let my mind consider the possibility that my parents were already dead, murdered in cold blood while I traveled across Oberia on a futile search for some mythical flower.

"I miss them too," I said, my voice wavering slightly. I could feel Darian's eyes studying me in the starlight, trying to read into my words to understand.

No one would ever understand the weight of carrying the lives of your parents, knowing their fate was in your hands.

We sat in silence in the crow's nest, gazing up at the sky, filled with shimmering stars.

"I've never seen the sky so big and open before," I whispered with awe. I had become accustomed to looking at the sky through a window or a canopy of trees in the forest surrounding the palace.

"It's beautiful, isn't it?" asked Darian. "There's something about being on the ocean that makes you realize how small you are. It's easy to get so used to your own little village that you forget there is a whole world out there."

I had often sat on the balcony adjoining my bedroom, staring at the cold stone of the palace walls and wondering what my life would be like if I wasn't the daughter of a king, heir to a crown and a country. I might have been a poor peasant girl, in love with her childhood playmate. I could have been born to a servant, a maid to the princess herself and grown up inside the palace, wishing for the very life I had now.

"Is everything alright?" asked Darian, interrupting my faraway thoughts.

I smiled wistfully, knowing it would do nothing to wish for a life that I could not have. "Yes, everything is fine," I replied. "Sometimes I just wonder what it would be like if things were different."

"You mean about coming on the *Maryanne*?" Darian questioned and I could tell he knew there was more going on than what I was saying.

"Not exactly...." I let my voice trail off as my words lingered in the cool night air. I wrapped my arms around my chest to try to keep warm.

"Here," said Darian, reaching beside him for a grey wool blanket. "I always keep a blanket with me for when I have the night shift. It does make it harder to stay awake though," he admitted with a chuckle.

I graciously accepted the extra warmth as he gently wrapped the blanket around my shoulders. "Thank you," I said, leaning back against the railing.

"Thank *you*," he replied. "The nights are always so long and it's nice to have company."

"Anytime. I have a lot on my mind so I wasn't planning on sleeping much anyways," I said, my quiet laughter echoing off the water below.

"Usually this shift gives me some time alone to think," Darian explained. "It can get overwhelming sometimes, always being around the same guys all day in small quarters. We get along for the most part but sometimes we have our disagreements."

"They're like your second family," I said. I felt the same way about the staff at the palace. I never grew up with siblings or cousins so the servant's children were my playmates and I'd known everyone there my whole life. Some of the staff who had worked there the longest were like grandparents to me.

"Yes, they are," agreed Darian. "I never had any siblings so the sailors are like my brothers."

I listened to his words with growing curiosity, intrigued by this boy who seemed so much like me.

"What?" asked Darian, staring at me with an unreadable expression.

"Nothing," I said, shaking myself out of my thoughts.

"Well, there obviously was something," he said, smiling. "What was going on in that mind of yours?"

I looked into his sea-green eyes, feeling a sudden urge to tell him everything about my family, about Draxon and the Rose. To be able to open up this boy and let him see the parts of me I had shut everyone else out of with my secrets and lies. The lies I had told to protect my heart and my identity.

It was exhausting trying to be Ari, an ordinary girl on her way to Destin, without a country or the lives of her parents resting on her. I let out a deep breath, pulling the blanket tighter around my shoulders.

"I was thinking about how wonderful it is to be here right now, sitting with you. It's so easy to forget all of my responsibilities and problems and just enjoy the night," I said, feeling my lips spread into a small smile.

"I feel exactly the same way," he said.

I looked away, feeling my heart skip a beat. I laid my head back against the railing and let the silence stretch between us. I could feel Darian's gaze on me, watching my eyes, my hair, my mouth.

My stomach fluttered and I tried not to think about the boy sitting beside me. I couldn't handle any distractions right now. In a few days, I would be getting off this ship and I would probably never see him again.

I felt my eyelids grow heavy and I let them close. I had barely slept since the day Draxon attacked the palace and took my parents hostage. My nights had been restless and filled with horrible thoughts about what Draxon had done to my family, about what he would do when I gave him the Rose. But tonight, I felt at peace, knowing I was exactly where I needed to be.

Draxon might have the upper hand in this situation but I knew for a fact he had underestimated the lengths I would go to save my parents and my people.

I had allowed myself to be the puppet on his string, the little girl he could manipulate into doing what he wanted but not anymore. I was severing my ties to this monster. I was the rightful heir to the kingdom of Oberia and I would not see it placed in his hands.

Chapter 6

"Ari," said a soft voice, a gentle hand shaking me awake. My eyelids fluttered and I blinked as faint rays of morning light shone in my eyes. Butterflies filled my stomach when I saw Darian's sea-green eyes gazing down at me. I felt the heat creep into my face as I realized I had fallen asleep with my head resting on his shoulder.

I sat up abruptly, running a hand through my hair which I imagined was sticking up in every direction.

"I didn't mean to fall asleep on you like that," I apologized, flustered.

"Not a problem," replied Darian with a grin. "I don't mind lending my shoulder for a pillow." He chuckled.

I felt my flush deepen at his words.

"Want to grab some breakfast?" he asked, standing and stretching his arms out with a yawn. "I'm starving."

"Sure," I said, graciously accepting the hand he offered to help me to my feet.

"Ladies first," he said, motioning to the ladder with a smirk.

"Thank you," I responded, sarcasm dripping off my tongue. I peered over the edge of the crow's nest to the deck below, eyeing the ladder with caution. It didn't seem nearly as high up as it had last night in the dark when I could barely make out the rungs beneath my feet. I turned around and began to descend the ladder, determined not to make a fool of myself again.

Darian stood at the top with his arms crossed over his chest, watching me with amusement.

I felt pride well up inside of me when my bare feet touched the deck.

"You managed to do it without squealing this time," said Darian, clapping his hands.

I dipped into a mock curtsy.

Darian climbed down the ladder after me with ease, jumping off a few rungs up and landing on his feet beside me with a thud.

"That's how it's really done," he said.

"Show off." I smirked.

Darian began to walk across the deck and I followed, eyeing the mist that hovered over the water. Sunlight streaked through the clouds, casting it's rays on the sides of the ship.

"I need to change before breakfast," I said, feeling self-conscious of my attire.

"Yes," agreed Darian, eyeing me with a smile. "That t-shirt was definitely more attractive in the dark."

I swatted his arm playfully, embarrassed by his remark. "I'll let Captain Carter know your thoughts on his shirt."

He let out a deep laugh, the smile spreading across his face and reaching his eyes. "Please do."

"I'll meet you in the kitchen in a few minutes," I said as we reached the stairs leading below deck.

"Okay," laughed Darian, casting a backwards glance over his shoulder as he headed down stairs.

I hurried across the deck to my makeshift room, my mind racing with thoughts of my conversation with Darian last night. There was so much I didn't know about him, so many secrets I wanted to find out, but I knew it wasn't my place. He was just another sailor on the *Maryanne* and once we reached Destin, we would both go our separate ways.

I felt a pang in my stomach at the thought of leaving the ship and going off on my own, even though that had always been the plan.

No one could ever know who I was or what I was really doing here without putting my life and my parents' at further risk.

The only person I could trust was myself.

I quickly changed into my clothes and ran my fingers through my hair, wishing I had a brush or something more presentable to wear. But now was not the time to be worrying about my appearance.

I desperately wished that life could go back to normal and I could forget this had ever happened. I missed worrying about what I would wear, when I would go riding, or if Mother would get me in trouble for not doing my schoolwork. I felt a twinge of guilt as I recognized my own selfishness. My parents were enduring far more than I had to and they were probably thinking about me and our people, not their own lives.

While many people thought being a royal meant living a life of privilege and luxury, rightfully so, they failed to realize that those same royals did not have the luxury of being selfish or moving in their own interests when the fate of a whole country laid in their hands.

Throughout history, many kings and queens had been overthrown by their subjects because they were power-hungry monsters who only thought of their own welfare when it came to making decisions. But my parents had never been those people. What scared me the most was that I knew my mother and father would sacrifice their own lives in a heartbeat if it meant my life and the lives of our people would be spared.

I ran one last hurried hand through my hair, attempting to smooth my unruly curls before leaving the room. For once I was thankful for the absence of a mirror because I knew I would be horrified if I saw what I had looked like to Darian this morning.

I walked down the stairs, smiling at the sound of laughter ringing from the kitchen. I heard the clank of mugs on the table top amid the friendly banter I was quickly growing accustomed to.

I scanned the room for Darian upon entering, catching sight of him seated at the kitchen table along with a few other men. He took a large swig of coffee, looking up to meet my gaze and giving a small wave in return. One of the men at the table who was seated across from Darian, his back to me, swiveled in his chair to see who was behind him.

The sight of Gabriel's hazel eyes made my heart skip a beat. *What was he doing here? Eating breakfast of course, just like all of the other sailors*, I chided myself. *But why did he have to sit with Darian?*

I felt a few nervous butterflies form in my stomach at the thought of Darian and Gabriel talking and getting to know each other. I wasn't sure why but the thought made me uncomfortable. I barely knew these boys and yet I worried how they would act around each other and around me.

Sucking in a deep breath, I walked over to the counter to grab myself a biscuit and a mug of coffee. Bracing myself for the awkward situation I had inevitably found myself in, I headed back over to the table where there was an empty chair beside Darian.

"I was starting to wonder if you had decided to skip breakfast," said Darian, pulling out the chair for me as I approached.

"No, I'm too hungry for that," I said with a laugh, looking at Gabriel to see his response.

His brow was drawn into a line as he looked between us, obviously wondering how we knew each other.

"Well you look more awake now than you did earlier," joked Darian with a wide grin.

My heart skipped a beat at his comment, not wanting Gabriel to get the wrong idea. "I couldn't sleep last night so I wandered out on the deck and ended up sitting with Darian in the lookout during his night shift," I explained in a rush of breath.

Gabriel cast me a questioning look, clearly not impressed with my explanation.

A tense silence hung between us and I took a bite of my cold biscuit, not sure what to say.

"How do you two know each other?" asked Darian, his curiosity evident in his voice.

Gabriel and I exchanged a glance and I attempted to swallow the bite lodged in the back of my throat.

"Well I was—" began Gabriel, just as I began to speak.

"We met—"

We both stopped and Gabriel motioned for me to go ahead.

"I was trying to find a ship headed to Destin and Gabriel was looking to get a job on the same ship so he helped me."

Darian nodded as I spoke but his eyes narrowed slightly at my words. He didn't seem fully convinced by my story.

"That was a pretty good coincidence for you," Darian said to me.

"Yeah it was," I said, forcing a chuckle. "I definitely would have missed the ship trying to find it on my own."

Gabriel and Darian stared at each other across the table and I could sense the tension rising.

"So what brings you to the *Maryanne*?" Gabriel asked Darian with a pointed look.

Darian leaned back in his chair and crossed his arms over his chest. "I've worked on this ship for the past two years. I needed a change from my village."

Gabriel nodded, thankfully not questioning him further. I watched his eyes wander to the frayed string on Darian's wrist where the violin pendant hung.

"Nice bracelet," he quipped, a mischievous grin spreading across his face. I gave him a hard kick under the table and he winced, turning to me with a frown.

"What was that for?"

I looked at him, warningly, trying to get him to drop the subject. I knew the bracelet meant a lot to Darian and I didn't want him to get hurt.

He looked at Gabriel and I thought I saw a flicker of anger pass over Darian's face. His sea-green eyes had turned a stormy grey and I laid a gentle hand on his arm to calm him.

"I'm sorry," I whispered. "Just ignore him."

"It was a simple question," snapped Gabriel. "You don't have to get all sensitive about it. It's only a dumb bracelet."

Darian leapt to his feet, throwing his chair back with a crash as it tumbled to the floor behind him. The other men had stopped their conversations to see the scene transpiring between the boys. I saw Darian's hands clenched into fists at his side, ready to punch Gabriel if he said one more thing.

My heart pounded in my chest and blood pounded furiously in my ears as I stood there, ready to jump between the two if they went at each other. I looked at Darian, desperately hoping he would back down before he started something they would both regret.

The silence hung heavy in the air as Darian and Gabriel stood facing one another. The table between them served as a barrier to prevent them from pummelling the other.

I let out a breath I hadn't known I was holding as I saw Darian relax his fists, stretching his fingers out and letting them fall back to his sides. He turned towards the door of the kitchen.

"I'm going to get some sleep," he said.

I could see the hurt in his eyes as he cast a final glance over his shoulder at me as I stood beside Gabriel.

My heart slowed its racing and I felt a lump form in my throat as I watched his retreating form. I felt as if I had betrayed Darian somehow, even though I had never chosen a side.

"What a loser," scoffed Gabriel with a smirk.

I glared at him, feeling anger building inside of me. "Don't you dare talk about him like that. You acted like a childhood bully by picking on him."

Out of the corner of my eye I noticed the other men begin to slip away, allowing us some privacy.

"What's going on between you two? Why are you suddenly defending him?"

"Nothing is going on between us," I spat. "He's a good guy and I don't appreciate you treating him that way."

"I only asked him a question," he protested.

"You know it wasn't just a harmless question. You wanted to make him mad but I don't understand why. You don't even know him."

"Neither do you."

"Well I don't really know you either," I retorted. "I thought I was starting to." I gave my chair a rough shove and stormed out of the room, leaving Gabriel alone.

"Darian," I called softly, peering in the doorway of the sailor's bunkroom. It was dark inside because there were no windows and I could only faintly make out the shape of the bunk beds lined up against the walls.

"Darian," I whispered again, making my way towards one of the beds on the far side of the room. I could make out the shape of someone curled up on the bottom bunk.

"What are you doing here?" asked Darian, sitting up abruptly.

I heard a dull thud as he banged his head against the top of the bunk above him.

"I do that every time," he said with a laugh, rubbing his head with his hand.

I let out a giggle. "I wanted to make sure you were okay," I said, my tone growing serious. "Gabriel had no right to treat you the way he did and I'm sorry. I have no idea what got into him."

"It's fine. I'm used to people making fun of it."

"That's no excuse," I replied. "Your mother gave it to you and it obviously means a lot."

He lowered his eyes at my words and I could tell he was trying to keep it together in front of me.

"I'll let you get some sleep," I said, after a long pause.

"Ari," said Darian softly. I felt him reach for my hand in the dark, catching me off guard. "Thanks again for last night. It meant a lot that you stayed up with me. It was nice to have someone to talk to for a change."

"Your welcome," I said, giving his hand a squeeze. "Anytime."

He let go of my hand and I stood beside him for a moment before turning to go. I tried to make sense of all the strange emotions whirling inside of me, knowing that Darian was unlike any boy I had ever met before. I felt like he understood me in a way no one else had. Being royalty had isolated me from all the other kids my age and now I was finally getting a chance to be known for who I really was instead of for my title and my family.

Now was not the time to be distracted though. I had a great responsibility and I would not let anything get in the way of that.

Or *anyone*.

Darian and Gabriel could never know who I was or what had brought me to the *Maryanne*. Because power had a way of corrupting even the purest hearts. If anyone found out who I was, there was no telling what they might do.

I didn't need another enemy.

Chapter 7

A few hours later, I found Gabriel mopping the upper deck, the hot afternoon sun beating down on him. A few of the other crew members worked nearby, sweeping and scrubbing the ship as they chatted.

"Ari," said Gabriel, looking up at me with his now familiar grin as I approached.

"Don't act like everything is okay," I snapped, stopping a few feet away from him. I had no idea what had gotten into Gabriel but at breakfast, he wasn't the playful, mischievous boy he normally appeared to be.

A frown lined his forehead and he leaned some of his weight on the mop he held in one hand.

"What's not okay?" he asked, raising an eyebrow in question.

I let out a huff of frustration and crossed my arms. "You know exactly what I'm talking about, Gabriel, so don't go playing the innocent game with me. You were purposely aggravating Darian and trying to start a fight. What is your problem?"

"Nothing," Gabriel said defensively, folding his arms over his chest to mirror my own position. "Darian is the one who got so worked up over a dumb bracelet."

I felt heat flush through my body, like fire running across a dry plain, turning everything in its path to ash.

"You don't know anything about Darian or what that bracelet means to him," I spat.

"And you do? Ari, you just met this boy and now all of a sudden you know everything about him? How do you know you can trust him?"

"I know that I don't know everything about him but I know more about his past than yours. And I'm beginning to wonder if I know you at all."

Silence fell between us and I felt the curious stares of the crew members as we stood across from each other. I lifted my jaw in defiance, my breath coming out in short, heavy bursts.

"Why are you on this ship?" Gabriel asked me, his eyes narrowing as he waited for my reply.

My stomach began to churn at his question and I could feel his eyes boring into mine, searching my heart for answers. I ducked my head and began to toy with a loose string that hung off the bottom of my shirt.

"That is none of your business, Gabriel, and it has nothing to do with what we're talking about. I asked you why you treated Darian the way you did and I want an answer."

"Calm down, Ari, I was only asking you a question. I realize I shouldn't have teased Darian about the bracelet since it's obviously important to him. I didn't think either of you would take it so seriously," he said, throwing his hands up in the air in frustration.

I scowled at him, not trusting the sincerity of his apology.

"Can we go somewhere and talk?" asked Gabriel, his tone possessing a pleading air to it.

"No, we have nothing to talk about," I replied, coldly.

"Yes we do. I don't like all the secrets between us and I think we need to talk about the real reason we are both here."

"I'm not keeping any secrets from you Gabriel, but feel free to share yours," I said, feeling my stomach tighten into a knot as I spoke. I couldn't open up to Gabriel, even though there was a small part of me that wanted to. I didn't know anything about him and there was no way I could tell him everything that was going on without putting my own life and the lives of my parents in even more jeopardy.

"Come on Ari, I know there's something going on and I want to know what it is."

"Leave me alone, Gabriel," I said, spinning on my heel and walking back towards my room.

Suddenly, a wave of icy water pummeled my back as soapy water ran down my neck and the sides of my face. I froze in shock, trying to process what had happened. I slowly turned around to face Gabriel, my hands clenched so tightly that my nails dug into the skin on my palms.

He was doubled over with laughter, holding his sides as his breath came out in short gasps. The empty bucket lay on the floor beside the tell tale puddles of soap and water.

Without thinking, I ran towards him, snatching up the mop that laid forgotten on the deck between us. I began to wave it in front of his face, watching with satisfaction as the soap and water sprayed all over him. A small giggle escaped my lips as Gabriel held up his arms to protect his face.

"Hey!" he cried.

"How does it feel?" I taunted him, shoving the mop in his face.

Gabriel grabbed my arms and I dropped the mop, letting it fall with a clatter to the deck between us. My heart skipped a beat as he looked at me with his hazel eyes, his playful smirk fading.

"I think we're even now," he said, his voice dropping as he spoke.

"Yes," I agreed, suddenly feeling the stares of the sailors watching our exchange.

Gabriel let go of my arms, his hands falling loosely at his sides. I grabbed the bottom of my shirt, wringing it out to form a small puddle on the deck.

"Looks like you'll have lots of mopping to do," I said, my eyes following the large pools of water spread across the deck.

I heard the chuckles of the rest of the crew as they picked up their own rags and brushes to resume their cleaning.

"Ari," said Gabriel softly, locking eyes with me again. "I want you to know that I am really sorry about this morning. I should never have treated you or Darian the way that I did. I'll make it up to you both."

"Okay," I whispered, a lump forming in the back of my throat. I desperately wanted to believe his promise.

Gabriel was the first to look away, leaning down to pick up the mop from off the deck.

"I guess I better fill up my bucket again," he said with a grin.

I picked the bucket up from where it laid on its side on the deck and handed it to him. I followed him across the ship to where there was a line of wooden barrels used to collect rain that we used for washing dishes and mopping the deck. An extra mop leaned up against the railing and I grabbed it.

"Looks like you could use a bit of help," I chirped.

"I'm doing just fine on my own," Gabriel protested.

"Clearly," I replied sarcastically, rolling my eyes and gesturing towards the puddles of soap and water running across the deck.

Gabriel began to scrub the deck furiously, attempting to remedy the mess he had made.

I laughed at the spectacle of a boy who had been a thief on the streets only a few days ago and was now mopping a ship deck.

"What an upgrade from your last form of employment," I said, teasingly.

The mischievous twinkle in Gabriel's eyes darkened and his smile faded. "Yes it is."

I felt my pulse quicken as I noted the dramatic shift in his tone.

"What brought you to the ship, Gabriel?" I prodded, gently, hoping to ease him into a conversation. I was intrigued by this mischievous boy and wanted to know his past.

Gabriel cast me a sideways glance and I watched his knuckles turn white as he gripped tighter to the mop handle.

"You."

My breath caught in the back of my throat at his boldness.

"What do you mean, *me?*" I stammered.

"I was surviving as best as I knew how, living on the streets and stealing to survive. You were just another victim of my pickpocket days. I never expected you to chase me down. No one has ever done that before."

"What made you give my things back?"

The slightest hint of a grin toyed at the corners of his lips. "I was shocked… and maybe a little impressed," he replied after a moment's hesitation.

I felt my stomach do a somersault at his words. "Impressed?" I said, giving Gabriel a small wink.

I watched with satisfaction as his cheeks turned pink with embarrassment.

"Why did you follow me to the ship?" I pressed, trying to find out more. Until now, Gabriel had been more than reluctant to open up to me and I wanted to know what had motivated his actions.

"You could have just left me alone after you gave my things back. What made you decide to follow me instead of finding someone else to pickpocket?"

Gabriel stopped mopping to look me in the eyes and I thought I caught the faintest glimmer of tears. "My life on the streets wasn't a life at all. I was surviving but I wasn't really living. When I saw you—" His voice became choked with emotion and he couldn't continue.

Instinctively, I reached out a hand and rested it on his shoulder. "I didn't mean to upset you, Gabriel."

"No, it's not you," he replied firmly. "I honestly don't know what made me follow you. I guess my curiosity got the best of me. And then when Captain Carter offered me a job on the ship I thought that maybe my luck was finally about to change, that maybe now I could finally start living."

His words hung in the air between us and I couldn't help but think about Draxon and his own motives. He had wasted years of his life consumed by rage and jealousy, wanting revenge and doing everything in his power to take the crown his brother had been handed. I wondered if he would ever look back and realize he had wasted the only life he had been given. Not even a magical flower could change that.

"Why are you on this ship, Ari? A girl like you who seems like she has the whole world at her fingertips must have a darn good reason for running away from it all."

I felt my chest constrict and I tried to take a deep breath but the air didn't seem to reach my lungs.

"What good is having the world at your fingertips if that world is falling apart and you're powerless to do anything about it?"

A strange look passed over Gabriel's face at my words and I wondered if I had said too much.

"And for your information," I continued, gritting my teeth tightly together, "I'm not running away."

Gabriel cocked his head sideways and looked me straight in the eyes. I could tell he didn't believe me.

"You can't say the same. You've already admitted you wanted to escape the streets and start fresh," I challenged him.

"You're right, Ari," Gabriel said with a shrug of his shoulders. "I am running away. But at least I'm not lying to myself about it."

Defiance bubbled up inside of me accompanied by a thousand snide retorts but I swallowed them all.

Gabriel had no clue what was going on in my life. He didn't know my parents were being held hostage by a power hungry monster who wanted them dead. He didn't know that the reason I was an ocean away from them wasn't my choice but because I had to find a magical flower in order to save their lives.

No. I wasn't running away. I was doing what I had to do to save my parents and my people.

But a sliver of doubt had wedged itself in my heart like a piece of glass. I was heir to the crown, future queen of Oberia and yet I was going to let my enemy tell me what to do? If I was a real princess, I would have stayed and fought for my family instead of giving in to Draxon's demands.

Leaving the palace and getting on a ship that would take me an ocean away was exactly what Draxon wanted me to do. Staying and fighting was the opposite.

"What if I am running?" I asked Gabriel, forcing myself to meet his penetrating gaze.

"You better know what—or who—you're running from."

I felt my stomach plummet to my feet. "Who are you running from, Gabriel?"

"I don't have anyone to run from," he answered abruptly.

"I don't believe you," I said. "Everyone has a monster they've locked away in their closet that they hope they'll never have to open again."

I watched Gabriel's face harden as I spoke. "I guess I'm one of the lucky ones then."

I shook my head, feeling tears of frustration well up in the backs of my eyes. I desperately wanted Gabriel to open up to me and let me in but it seemed he only wanted to keep everyone out. When he locked his monsters away, he locked away his friends too.

"You can point fingers at me all you want, Gabriel. You can tell me I'm living in denial and lying to myself about running away from my problems. But you're running from something too. Let me know when you get tired of believing your own lies." I threw the mop to the side of the deck and walked away.

This time, Gabriel didn't try to follow me.

Chapter 8

I sat at the kitchen table with my head in my hands, blinking back the tears that burned the backs of my eyes as everyone cleared away the dinner dishes to make room for a game of cards. I hadn't spoken to Gabriel since yesterday afternoon but his words still rang in my ears no matter how hard I tried to forget them.

A girl like you who seems like she has the whole world at her fingertips must have a darn good reason for running away from it all.

When I left Aurora, I had thought I was doing the right thing, the only thing there was to do. But now I wasn't so sure. I felt like I had failed my kingdom and was running away from my enemy instead of fighting back.

But who was I to go up against a monster like Draxon?

I heard the scraping of a chair against the hardwood and I jerked my head up in alarm to see Captain Carter take a seat across from me at the table.

I held a hand to my chest and sucked in a deep breath. "You startled me," I said, forcing a lighthearted laugh.

Captain Carter looked at me with concern. "Is everything alright, Ari? I don't pretend to know what has brought you to this ship but it seems like you have a lot going on. Is there anything I can help with?"

"Everything's fine," I lied, looking down at my hands.

"Ari," Captain Carter said sternly, "I know you're not being honest with me. I won't force you to tell me but I will say that I saw your little water fight with Gabriel and then you walked away looking upset. If he's bothering you, I can talk to him."

"No," I said quickly, "it's not Gabriel at all."

Captain Carter cast me another worried look. "You can tell me you know. I want everyone to feel comfortable and at home on my ship."

"Thank you," I said sincerely, looking up at him from the table. "I really do appreciate everything you have done for me. But there's nothing more you can do for me than you already have."

Captain Carter leaned back in his chair with a heavy sigh. "I might be overstepping here but I don't think it's a good idea for you to get off at Destin alone. Would you consider letting Gabriel or another crew member accompany you to wherever it is that you're going?"

"I know you're concerned, Captain, but I am perfectly capable of taking care of myself. I will be fine on my own."

"So I take that as a no then?" asked Captain Carter, his brow furrowing.

I forced myself to nod, refusing to argue with him about this. I needed to do this on my own. I wasn't going to drag anyone else into this mess or risk putting my family in any more danger.

"If that's how you want it then," Captain Carter said reluctantly. "I wish you would reconsider or at least mention the idea to Gabriel."

I didn't reply. If I asked, I was sure Gabriel would say yes and I didn't want him following me around anymore. This was his chance at a fresh start and I would not ruin that for him.

"In three days we will arrive in Destin so you have until then to make your decision."

Three days. That's all the time I had left until the real journey would begin. Leaving the palace had been hard but leaving Darian would be like leaving behind a piece of my heart, knowing I would never get it back.

We sat at the table in awkward silence for a few minutes, listening to the sound of the sailor's raucous laughter and the clanking of dishes.

"Are you sure there is nothing you want to tell me?" Captain Carter prodded me again.

"Thank you for your concern but everything is okay," I said, forcing myself to smile.

I knew Captain Carter could see right through my little act but I didn't care. I couldn't risk telling him the truth.

He sat at the table for another long moment before getting up to leave. "I'll let you be alone if that's what you want," he said.

As I watched him disappear through the doorway, I realized that maybe I had locked away more than just my monsters. I had pointed fingers at Gabriel for shutting me out but I had done the same thing to him and to Captain Carter.

But my situation was different. I couldn't tell anyone what was going on.

Draxon's spoon fed lies blended with my own reasoning and logic until I couldn't distinguish between my own fear and the right thing to do.

An uneasy feeling filled my stomach and I wondered if by doing what I had thought was right, I had allowed myself to walk right into Draxon's trap.

"Hey Ari," called Darian from across the room. "Are you up for a game of cards?"

I debated saying no but I really didn't want to be alone with my thoughts and regrets.

"Sure, if you can handle the competition," I quipped, forcing a smile.

"Is that a challenge I hear?" asked Darian with a smirk.

The sailors joined in on my laughter as I made my way over to the table and took a seat across from Darian.

I made eye contact with Gabriel as he tilted his head back and took a swig of whiskey out of the bottle. He nonchalantly picked up the deck of cards and dealt each person a hand.

I reached for the middle pile and my fingers brushed Gabriel's as he reached for the same one. Our eyes locked as his hand rested on top of mine.

Out of the corner of my eye I saw Darian watching us.

Wordlessly, I pulled my hand out from under his and grabbed the pile of cards beside it.

"I never thought you would be one to back down first from something you want. Usually you always get your way," said Gabriel with a smirk.

I snatched the bottle of whiskey out of his hand and took a large gulp, feeling the burn as the liquid trailed down my throat.

"I know when something is worth the fight," I replied in an icy tone.

I felt the tension rising in the small room as the other men studied their cards intently, trying to ignore the scene transpiring before them.

The men began playing cards and betting chips but Gabriel never took his eyes off me.

I leaned back in my chair with a smirk as I watched the growing pile of chips on the battered wooden table, the stakes quickly rising in my favour.

I eyed the half empty glass of whiskey Gabriel held in his right hand, his left clutching tightly to his hand of dog-eared playing cards. He ran a tense hand through his mop of dark brown hair and leaned back in his chair.

I looked down at my own cards, measuring the stakes. "I'm all in," I said, shoving the rest of my chips to the center of the table. I had nothing left to lose.

"You sure you want to do that, Ari?" said Gabriel with an arch of his brows. "You don't know what cards everyone else is holding."

"I don't need to," I said, with a smirk.

Darians's brow furrowed and his eyes flitted between the two of us, trying to read into our conversation.

"Okay," Gabriel said, after a moment of tense silence.

My heart beat quickened as he pushed all of his chips into the center of the table.

"I guess I'm all in too."

Darian choked on his drink, beginning to cough and sputter. The man beside him gave him a hard slap on the back.

"You okay Darian? Maybe you should sit this game out," said Gabriel in a mocking tone. A sly grin spread across his face as he watched me squirm uncomfortably in my seat.

"I'm fine," snapped Darian. "Thank you for your concern," he growled.

"Alright, who's the lucky winner," said the man next to me with a scraggly red beard, throwing down an empty hand of cards.

One by one, each man threw down an empty hand.

Darian looked at me across the table before laying down his hand. Empty. I sucked in a deep breath before watching Gabriel lay down his hand with a gleeful smile. A straight.

He gave me a coy wink and crossed his arms over his chest, waiting for me to reveal my hand. As all eyes turned to me, I slowly laid down my hand beside Gabriel's.

There was a heavy silence as everyone looked from my cards to the pile of chips in the center.

"Full house," exclaimed Gabriel, slamming his glass on the table, whiskey sloshing over the side onto the table.

I stood up in triumph, scooping up the chips as the other men looked at me with shock.

"Who knew the lass could kick butt at cards?" he said with a chuckle.

Gabriel glanced up at me from where he leaned back in his chair. "I did."

"You did not," I retorted as I threw a chip at him. "Or else you wouldn't have gone all in."

"What if I did?"

My laughter subsided as I stared into his dark hazel eyes.

"Just because you lose one game doesn't mean you lose them all," he said.

Around us, the other sailors were getting ready to play another game, refilling their glasses with whiskey and dealing out the cards.

"You want to play another game, Ari?" asked one of the sailors.

"No, I think I'll sit this one out," I said, standing up and pushing in my chair.

Gabriel stood up to follow me. "Count me out too," he said.

I cast a glance at Darian who was watching us, his cheeks flushed with anger. He stood abruptly, his chair screeching against the wood floor.

"Leave her alone, Gabriel. She doesn't want you anywhere near her," Darian spat.

"Woah there, settle down," said Gabriel, raising his hands in playful surrender. "I'm not doing anything wrong here. Just because you're jealous and don't want me around Ari doesn't mean that's what she wants. Let the lady speak for herself." He turned to me with that boyish smile of his and waited for my reply.

I stammered, my gaze flickering between Gabriel and Darian. I was still upset with Gabriel from our fight yesterday afternoon but there was a tiny part of me that did want to talk to him and figure things out.

He seemed like a completely different boy than the one who I had jumped only a few days ago at the wharf when he stole my compass. Now, I didn't know what to make of him.

"I'll only be a minute," I promised Darian, hoping he could read the apology in my eyes.

Darian blinked, letting his fists unclench and his arms fall helplessly to his side.

He slumped back down in his chair and accepted another hand of cards. "Maybe I'll have some better luck this game," he said, turning his back to us.

I left the kitchen wordlessly, hearing Gabriel's footsteps behind me. I kept walking until we reached the upper deck, stopping to stand at the railing. The moon was a small sliver in the dusky sky as the sunset faded to grey.

"Where did you learn to play cards?" asked Gabriel, resting his elbows on the edge of the railing.

My mind wandered to the countless nights I had spent down in the kitchen at the palace, playing cards with the servants when I was supposed to be in bed.

"Lets just say my parents wouldn't approve," I said, with a small smile.

"You played a fair game though," he said with a chuckle. "There aren't many honest players out there."

"I guess not," I replied, laughing.

I could feel Gabriel's eyes resting on me and he sucked in a breath, hesitating before he spoke.

"I meant what I said about being all in," he said.

"What do you mean?" I asked, confusion clouding my mind and my heart.

"I know we've gotten off on the wrong foot... multiple times," he said sheepishly. "But I want you to give me a chance."

"What are you talking about, Gabriel," I asked, brushing a loose strand of hair out of my eyes. "Get to the point."

"When we dock in Destin, I want to get off the ship with you."

All the angry words, all the arguments, all the reasons why this was a terrible idea fled my mind and I stood in front of Gabriel, grasping for the right thing to say.

"Say something," he said, clasping and unclasping his hands repeatedly as he waited for me to respond.

"I honestly don't know what to say," I said, truthfully. "I should say no."

"But do you want to?"

I let the silence drag between us. I thought I wanted to say no. Now that Gabriel was standing in front of me, I didn't know if I could.

"Gabriel, I—"

My breath caught in my throat, choking my words back down as Gabriel leaned forward and pressed his lips against mine.

Shock and confusion washed over me and I froze, letting myself feel Gabriel's lips against mine, his hand on my cheek and the other reaching up into my hair.

The realization of what was happening hit me and I immediately pulled away from him, trying to put as much space between us on the deck as I could.

"Ari, I'm sorry, I shouldn't have been so bold. I just—"

"Don't talk to me," I said, my hands trembling as I reached up to press my fingers against my lips, as if I could erase the feeling of Gabriel's lips on mine.

"I have to go." I turned my back to him and began to walk as fast as I could down the deck towards my bedroom.

"There you go, running away again," exclaimed Gabriel, throwing his hands up in the air in exasperation. "No matter how far you run, it doesn't change anything, Ari. This kiss happened tonight whether you deny it or not."

"I didn't ask for you to kiss me, Gabriel," I cried, stopping in my tracks to face him, hating the tears that began to fall down my cheeks. "I didn't ask for you to come with me or to be my friend. I didn't ask for any of this. I left home for one reason and one reason only and you are ruining everything."

In the light of the moon I could see Gabriel's face pinch with anger and his eyes grow dark.

"When are you going to stop trying to control everything and let things happen when they are meant to happen? You can't decide when you're going to love someone or even choose who that person is going to be. It happens on its own."

"Is that what you think this is?" I asked with a cold chuckle. "Love?" My voice grew hoarse as I spoke. "Gabriel, I don't know what this is but it certainly isn't love. I barely even know you. You stole from me, you have insulted me more times than I can count, you look down on me and we fight all the time."

"Ari, please, you don't even know me—"

"Exactly, you don't know me either," I continued, "and you never will. I'm done with this conversation, Gabriel. In three days I will be getting off this ship alone so I can do what I came to do. I don't need anyone's help, least of all, *yours*." With my words still ringing in the air, I spun on my heel, leaving Gabriel alone on the deck as I ran to my room and slammed the door behind me.

I flopped down on my cot and stared up at the ceiling, letting the tears stream down my face. Gabriel's words rang in my ears and the feeling of his lips pressed against mine sent me into a spiral of panic. This couldn't be happening right now. The last thing I needed in the middle of everything that was going on was to get my heart attached to a guy I could never have.

I let my thoughts wander to the memory of the night I had spent in Darian's arms. The night where I was just a girl with a boy. A boy who listened to me and understood me. Who wanted to learn to see the world through my eyes, not just his own.

The feeling of his body against mine and his breath, soft and low beside me sent a flutter of butterflies racing through my stomach.

I had only just met Darian but I knew he was different. When I was with him, everything else in my world faded into the background and it was only us. He didn't force me to be anyone else but he didn't let me hide the person I was. Darian wanted to know me. And I wanted to know him.

I knew the right thing to do would be to let him go. But I didn't want to. Letting him go meant letting go of a piece of my heart when I left. There was no alternative. Entertaining this fantasy that things could be any different would only cause us both more pain in the end. But shutting him out would take more strength than I had.

My heart was in a game of tug of war and I was caught in the middle, unsure which side to choose. But now wasn't the right time. I was a servant to my crown and the only way to save it was by finding the Red Rose. Finding love was not in the cards for me. Not now and maybe not ever.

A dull, hollow ache formed in my chest and my body began to tremble. I felt as if the room was closing in on me, trapping me in the cage I had blindly walked into.

Gasping for air, I jumped out of bed and ran for the door. I blinked rapidly, trying to clear my blurring vision as I fumbled to find the door handle. My hand wrapped around it and I pushed, falling out of the closet and onto the deck with a thud.

I scrambled to my feet and began to run along the deck, listening to my ragged breathing in the quiet night air and the blood thundering in my ears.

I didn't know where I was going but when I felt my foot hit the first rung of the ladder, I let my body lead my heart to where it needed to be.

As I neared the top, I heard *him* say my name and I felt the tears pour hot and fast down my cheeks. Darian's strong arms wrapped around me and I stood there, holding on to the one person I knew I could never let go of.

I leaned my head against his chest and felt the gentle rhythm of his heart beating against mine. *One, two, three.* Over and over, beat after beat. It was crazy to think about how much could change in a single heartbeat.

"Darian," I whispered, wrapping my arms tighter around him.

"What's wrong, Ari?" he said, his breath tickling my ear as he ran his fingers through my hair.

I let out a deep shuddering breath and pulled away to look up into his eyes. "Everything's okay now."

Darian searched my gaze for the truth. "Ari, you can't keep pushing your problems to the side every time you find a temporary fix for them."

My heart skipped a beat. *A temporary fix.* I opened my mouth to speak but my words faltered as I choked back a sob.

"Let's talk about this," murmured Darian, taking my hand and leading me to the spot we had sat only a few nights ago when I had fallen asleep in his arms.

We sat down together and I resisted the urge to lay my head on his shoulder again. I couldn't allow myself to get comfortable around him when we would soon have to say goodbye.

"I wish things could be different," I whispered.

"You keep saying that," said Darian, "but I don't understand why they can't be. Ari, you are in control of your own life. If you want things to be different, you have the power to change them."

I wrapped my arms around myself, trying to keep from shivering in the cold night air. "Don't lie to me, Darian," I replied. "We all wish we could change the way things are but sometimes, things are just beyond our control."

"I don't believe that," he said, firmly. "We always have a choice."

"I didn't choose to come on this ship," I said, letting the words slip past my lips.

Darian cocked a sideways glance at me, waiting for me to go on. I felt my stomach do a flip flop but I knew I had to tell him the truth. It was too late to take the words back now.

"I haven't been entirely honest with you, Darian. I want to let you in…." I let my voice trail off before gathering my courage to continue. "But I'm scared."

Darian cupped my chin in his callused hands and I could see the kindness in his eyes.

"I know you're scared, Ari. But know that I would never do anything to hurt you."

I ducked my head and his hands slipped away. I wanted to believe him. But there was a part of me that just couldn't.

"It's about time I told you the truth about why I'm on this ship, Ari," said Darian.

I felt my stomach fill with nervous butterflies. "I don't want to force you to let me in."

"I want to let you in," he murmured. He hesitated, staring off into the distance at the dark horizon before us.

"My mother was born into a wealthy family and her parents didn't approve of my father. She got pregnant out of wedlock and was sent away to have me and then forced to give me up. I never got to meet either of my parents."

My heartbeat quickened, watching Darian's face intently for any flicker of emotion. His face was as cold as stone and his eyes hardened as he spoke.

"All I have of my mother is this bracelet that my father gave her before she was sent away." I heard the tremor in Darian's voice and I watched as the walls that he had built crumbled at his feet, revealing the hollow shell of a boy who had kept his past locked away for far too long.

I took my hand and placed it gently over his. I watched as my small hand entwined with his bigger one, fitting perfectly together.

Darian's gaze flickered to our hands and he gave mine a gentle squeeze.

"I'm not angry about what happened," he continued. "I was brought up by a kind, loving couple who weren't able to have children of their own. But questions plagued me growing up about who my real parents are and what happened to them. So when I turned sixteen, I decided to leave home and find out for myself. All I want is to be able to meet them," he said, his voice dropping off as he spoke.

My heart broke at the thought of my own parents and what it would have been like to have been given up at birth and to never get the chance to see them face to face.

"So you've been trying to find your parents for the past two years?" I asked in disbelief.

He nodded. I've been all over Oberia trying to find them and asking people if they know anything about them. My mother's name is Madeline and my father's name was Jack but I don't know anything about either of them or what family they were from. I don't even know if they are alive. If I'm honest, I've given up on ever meeting them. That's why I'm on this ship. I broke my family's heart when I left them and I don't know if I can face them again."

A heavy silence fell over us like an iron cage, trapping us in prison's of our own making. We both had secrets we had kept from each other and had shut everyone out.

"You don't have to say anything, Ari," said Darian, looking up to meet my gaze, "I just thought you should know."

All of my walls came crashing down around me and I found myself in his arms, hugging him and never wanting to let go. He was my safe place and I was his.

Gut wrenching sobs tore through my body as I clung to him, feeling like I had failed my parents. Here was a boy who loved his parents that he had never even met and would do anything to find them while I had left mine behind under the captivity of a man who wanted them dead. I hadn't fought back or tried to get help. I left them alone and now I didn't even know if they were dead or alive. And whatever happened to them was all my fault.

"What's really going on, Ari?" Darian whispered, his breath tickling my ear.

"I left my parents to die," I cried between hiccups, unable to catch my breath.

"What are you talking about?" asked Darian, pulling away to cup my chin with his hand and brushing away the tears that streamed down my face.

"My uncle is holding my parents hostage and in exchange for their lives I have to find a mythical Red Rose. I should have stayed and fought back but instead I ran like a coward and now I'm not even sure if my parents are alive," I gasped out.

Darian's eyes widened with alarm and he opened his mouth to speak but quickly shut it again. He pulled me close and wrapped his arms around me once more.

"Ari, you can't blame yourself for this and I know your parents don't either. You are doing the right thing by trying to save them and fighting back might have put your parents at further risk."

"But what if he made up everything about the Red Rose as a way to get me out of the way so he could kill my parents? Or what if he doesn't hold up his end of the deal and kills my parents after I give him the Rose?" I asked, my voice rising with anger as I spoke.

"I honestly don't know, Ari, but I want to help. Let me help you," Darian begged.

My heart skipped a beat and I wondered if he could feel my heart pounding against his.

"No," I said firmly, pulling away from him and letting my hands fall empty at my side. Every part of me wanted to say yes but I couldn't let him do it.

"You are on this ship for a reason Darian, and it isn't to help me. You need to find your parents. I am not going to be responsible for you missing out on something you have waited your whole life for. I don't want to be your biggest regret." Another tear escaped my eye and dripped down my cheek.

I could feel Darian's eyes resting on me and he sucked in a breath. There was no hesitation in his voice when he spoke.

"If I let you go, you might be my biggest regret."

Fear gripped me, wrapping an iron fist around my lungs and squeezing until there was no breath left. Fear of being loved. Fear of loving someone I could never have. Or someone I could.

"Ari, you're different from anyone I have ever met. I want to know you, the *real* you. Not the perfect, put together girl you pretend to be in front of everyone else," Darian continued.

My heart began to race and blood pounded furiously in my ears, drowning out everything else around me except his deep, soft voice.

"I hope I'm not crossing a line by saying this because I know we only just met. I know you have secrets and I have mine too. But you don't have to hide them from me." He let out a deep breath I knew he had been holding in. I could tell there was more he wanted to say but he resisted the urge.

"Say something," he whispered, watching me in the darkness.

"You definitely crossed a line," I said, my heart skipping a beat.

His face fell and I watched his fingers fiddle with the violin pendant around his wrist.

"But I'm glad you did," I murmured.

His eyes widened with surprise and he took a step closer to me. "You mean that?"

"If I'm totally honest, I'm terrified to let anyone see that girl, the imperfect one, the one with secrets she's never told anyone before. But I want you to know her."

I felt Darian's gentle hand on my cheek while his other one reached up to brush a loose strand of hair out of my eye.

"I want to know her too."

I could feel the breath from his words, warm and sweet on my face and then his lips were against mine.

In that moment, a thousand questions, worries and fears faded to the back of my mind and everything felt right.

Draxon was still my enemy and my battle against him was far from over.

But for once, I felt like I had finally won something worth winning.

Chapter 9

Dusk had fallen and I sat on the cot in my room, looking at the map Draxon had given me for the hundredth time. Only two more days until we arrived in Destin. I desperately hoped I would not return home empty handed and that Draxon would hold up his end of the deal. I wanted to believe that this time, he would be a man of his word.

I jumped at the sound of a knock at the door. Before I had the chance to reply, the door flew open and Gabriel stalked in. I slowly got to my feet, leaving the map on my cot.

"What are you doing here? How dare you barge in like that?" I exclaimed, blood rushing to my head and pounding furiously in my ears.

"I knocked, didn't I?" Gabriel chirped back with a glare. His hazel eyes darkened as he held my gaze.

"Get. Out," I growled through clenched teeth, giving him a rough shove towards the door.

"Order me around all you want, Ari, I'm not leaving until I say what I came to say," Gabriel said, firmly.

I crossed my arms. "I'm tired of your games, Gabriel. You think you can come on this ship and follow me around and I'm just going to fall all over you but you're lying to yourself. I see right through your little act."

"And what *act* might that be?" he asked, eyes flashing.

"The one where you pretend to be a gentleman with that charming smile and smooth talk," I said, my voice rising as I spoke.

"Admit it, Ari, you melt whenever I give you that smile," Gabriel said, with a cold chuckle.

"You're so full of yourself," I retorted.

"At least I have confidence. You walk around this ship every day like a lost little girl who needs her parents."

I ground my teeth tightly together and dug my nails into my palms until they throbbed. Tears blurred my vision but I blinked them back.

"Leave," I choked out.

"I haven't said what I came to say yet," said Gabriel, smirking at my discomfort. "I'll leave when I'm ready."

"You'll leave when I tell you too and you've said more than enough."

"I was right about your parents," he said, taking a step closer to me in the small room. "I can see it in your eyes, Ari. You're trying to run away from your problems."

My heart slammed in my chest, each beat coming faster and harder than the last. "You don't know anything about me, Gabriel, or my problems. I never asked you to come here, to help me or befriend me or whatever it is that you're trying to do," I said, throwing my arms up in the air in exasperation.

"I needed a job and Captain Carter offered me one, so I took it," he replied, coolly.

"Why were you on the streets, Gabriel?" I asked, straightening up so our eyes were level with each other. "What happened to your mother?" I pressed.

I saw a glimmer of tears in his eyes. "You're the one who is really running away, aren't you?"

"I'm not running away," spat Gabriel, the dark, hollow look I'd seen in his eyes after the fight with Darian returning.

"Then why are you here? Why were you so rude to Darian the other day? Why will you not leave me alone?" I cried.

Garbriel took a step back. "I'm leaving," he said.

Rage burned inside of me, as if someone had thrown kerosene on an open fire. I grabbed Gabriel's arms, catching him by surprise, and shoved him against the shelves in the storage room.

"You started this and you're going to finish it," I said, angrily. "I want answers and you're not leaving until I get them."

I stood there, looking into Gabriel's flushed face as his chest rose and fell rapidly with each breath.

"My mother is dead," he said, quietly, the fight immediately leaving his eyes. "Is that what you wanted to hear, Ari? My mother is dead and my father squandered all our money on drink. He would stagger in from the tavern in the middle of the night, throwing furniture around and cursing. He was always angry and liked to use his fists more than he did words. A life on the streets was more of a life than that. My mother was the only reason I stayed as long as I did." A single tear slid from the cold, hollow abyss of Gabriel's eyes.

"I'm sorry," I whispered, tasting salt on my lips.

Gabriel brushed at his eyes, looking down at the cot below his feet. His eyes fell on the map I had thrown there when he came in. He reached down to pick it up and I didn't stop him.

"So, you're not running away?" asked Gabriel, his brows knitting together as he studied the faded, yellow cloth.

Dozens of lies came into my mind but I knew I couldn't lie to Gabriel any longer. He had opened up to me about his past and it was time to let him see mine. "I had no choice," I said, my voice catching in my throat.

"There's always a choice," replied Gabriel with a far away look in his eyes. "It just depends on what the alternative is."

"Well, letting my parents be murdered is not an alternative I'm willing to consider."

Gabriel looked up at me, his eyes widening with shock.

"My uncle will kill my parents if I don't get him some mythical Rose that is said to possess magical powers," I explained, leaving out any mention of my family's royal background or Draxon's claims on the throne.

I studied Gabriel's face intently, watching for his reaction. He would probably think I was insane.

His gaze clouded and his lips were drawn together in a firm, tight line. A heavy silence fell between us. My eyes fell on the map which shook ever so slightly in Gabriel's hands.

"Why?" he asked, looking up at me with wide eyes. I could see a faint sheen of sweat on his upper lip.

"Because he is a power-hungry monster who will do whatever it takes to get what he wants," I said, my heart beginning to race.

Gabriel shook his head. "No, why *you*?" he asked. "Why couldn't Draxon find someone else to get the Rose for him?"

I swallowed around the lump that had formed in my throat. "It's complicated."

"How can it be complicated?" Gabriel said, his voice rising in volume. "If all Draxon wants is the Rose, then he could have chosen anyone to get it for him. But he chose you."

Sucking in a deep breath, I slowly pulled down the sleeve of my shirt on my left arm, revealing the mark I had kept hidden since birth. Only my parents and Draxon knew it existed. And now Gabriel.

I saw his eyes narrow with confusion as he took in the red mark on my shoulder, shaped like a rose.

"What is this?" Gabriel asked, looking up at me.

My heartbeat quickened as he reached out and laid his hand on the mark. His hand was warm against my skin which had grown strangely cold. He traced the petals with his finger, causing a shiver to run down my spine.

After what felt like an eternity, Gabriel pulled his hand away and let it fall back to his side. I quickly pulled my sleeve up to cover the mark, feeling as if I had just given away a piece of myself.

"Do you believe the Rose is real?" asked Gabriel, looking at me somberly.

"I don't know what I believe anymore," I said, throwing my hands up in the air in frustration. "I don't know who I can trust, that's why I've kept everything a secret—until now."

Except my identity. That I could never reveal. If people knew I was the princess, heir to the Oberian throne, my life could be in danger.

Gabriel began to back away towards the door, his face suddenly losing all its colour.

"Where are you going? Is everything okay?" I asked, worriedly.

"I'm so sorry, Ari, I have to go. It's my turn to take the night shift."

Confusion filled me as he flung the door open. "So that's it then? That's the end of the conversation? We're not going to talk about the Rose or the mark on my arm or about my family? We're not going to talk about your past? Or how about when you kissed me last night and told me you wanted to get off the ship with me?"

"There's nothing to discuss," Gabriel said, turning his back to me.

"I think we have a lot to talk about." I heard someone say.

My stomach lurched as I caught sight of Darian's tall, broad-shouldered figure standing in the doorway, his arms crossed over his chest.

I saw Gabriel's body tense up as he took a step backwards towards me.

"What is going on Ari?"

"How long have you been standing there for? What did you hear?" I questioned, my voice tinted with suspicion. Darian had no right to eavesdrop on my personal conversation. What I told Gabriel was none of his business.

"Just long enough to hear you say that he kissed you? Was this before or after *our* kiss?" he asked, his voice rising angrily.

"You kissed Darian?" accused Gabriel with disbelief.

I felt my chest constrict as I looked between the two men standing before me. My breath came out in short gasps and I had no idea what to say.

"Get out."

"What?" said Darian, taking a step closer to me.

"Both of you. Get out of my room right now."

"I thought you wanted to talk," sneered Gabriel, obviously changing his mind about leaving now that Darian had showed up.

"I'll talk to you, Gabriel," chirped Darian. Without warning, he charged at Gabriel, one hand clenched into a tight fist that slammed into the side of his head with a sickening thud. Gabriel staggered backwards, caught off guard. I screamed as I ran for Darian, grabbing the back of his shirt and trying to pull him away. Gabriel came back with his own fists, thrusting one into Darian's nose and then his chest.

With a furious roar, Darian grabbed the collar of Gabriel's shirt and shoved him against the shelves lining the back of the tiny room. A bunch of boxes crashed to the floor beside them, one barely missing Gabriel's head.

"Stop it!" I exclaimed, furiously.

"What is the meaning of this?" came Captain Carter's stern voice. Two sailors rushed into the room and grabbed hold of Gabriel and Darian, trying to separate them.

"I will not tolerate this kind of behaviour on my ship," he said, a deep frown crossing his face.

I could feel my hands trembling as I backed away from Gabriel and Darian who were being held by the sailors.

"I don't want to talk about it," I said quietly. "Just get these guys out of my room," I snapped.

Captain Carter studied me intently for a moment before motioning to the sailors to take Gabriel and Darian away. "I'll let you be, Ari. But if you want to talk about it later after you've had a chance to calm down, let me know."

I nodded, choosing not to speak. I didn't trust my voice right now.

I waited until everyone had left the room and the door was shut tightly behind them before collapsing on the floor.

How had everything gone so horribly wrong? I had opened up to both Gabriel and Darian since I had boarded this ship and all they had caused me was trouble. It seemed like there was a rift between them and I had no idea why. They didn't even know each other.

The image of Darian's face, tense with anger flashed through my mind. The first thing he had asked about was the kiss. *Was he jealous that Gabriel had kissed me?* He had confessed that he had feelings for me and it seemed like Gabriel did too.

In a few days I would be leaving them both behind and this would all be in the past. There was a part of me that didn't want to leave, a part of me that wanted to give Darian a chance and see what the future might hold for us.

But I wasn't even sure if I had a future. If I returned home empty-handed, Draxon would kill me and my parents—if he hadn't already.

There was no place in my life for a boy, least of all one I had only met a few days ago. The best place to leave Darian was in the past. All he could ever be to me was a memory.

I felt a small twinge in the pit of my stomach at the thought of never seeing Darian—or Gabriel, again.

I got to my feet, brushing off my clothes and smoothing my hair. I was the heir to the Oberian throne and I would not let myself fall apart over a boy. No matter how much he meant to me. I would get off this ship when we docked in Destin. Alone. And I would do what I had come to do.

Darian and Gabriel would move on and so would I.

Chapter 10

"Why me?" I choked out. A lump formed in the back of my throat as I stood at the kitchen sink, washing dishes from lunch.

I had been tiptoeing around the ship since the incident with Darian and Gabriel yesterday. I didn't want to talk to them. I had trusted them and they had let me down.

Tomorrow morning we would be arriving in Destin and I wasn't ready. For the first time since I left the palace, I would be all alone with no one to turn to.

I didn't feel like the courageous, selfless daughter everyone thought me to be when I had left my home behind. Really, I was a coward who was too afraid to stand up to Draxon. I had chosen to believe his lies, to believe that obedience to a monster was what would save my parents.

But I knew that wasn't the truth.

Draxon did whatever it took to ensure I would be far away from Aurora so he could kill my parents and take over the kingdom without me there to cause trouble.

I began to shake uncontrollably and the plate I was drying slipped from my hands and fell to the floor with a crash. It shattered into a thousand tiny pieces.

I slumped down beside the counter and laid my head in my hands, feeling the pin pricks of glass digging into my skin.

My body shuddered thoughts whirling in my mind about what would become of my parents if I failed. What would become of my kingdom and my country. They would all break under Draxon's iron rule.

I didn't know what the right thing to do was anymore.

The sound of footsteps crunching on glass startled me and I looked up. My heart skipped a beat as my eyes met Darian's. He reached out a hand towards me and waited for me to take it.

"Get away from me," I managed to croak out, my voice hoarse from crying. "I don't want to talk to you."

"Ari," murmured Darian softly. "Look at me." He slowly knelt down in the glass beside me and lifted my chin with my hand. He gently brushed a wisp of hair out of my eyes and tucked it behind my ear.

My heart caught in my throat and all my anger slipped away when I looked into Darian's eyes.

"I never wanted to hurt you. I know I was a jerk to you and to Gabriel yesterday and I'm so sorry. Please forgive me?"

I nodded slowly as a tear slid down my cheek and dripped onto my neck. I couldn't find the words to speak.

A whisper of a smile tugged at the corner's of Darian's mouth and he reached out a hand to me. Wordlessly, I took his hand in mine and let him pull me to my feet, wincing as I felt little pieces of glass dig themselves into my skin.

Darian gently led me over to the table and pulled out a chair for me to sit on before pulling out one for himself and taking a seat across from me.

We looked at each other across the table and I could see the questions in Darian's eyes as he studied me intently.

"Please don't ask about the plate," I said.

"That was a plate?" he asked with a teasing smirk. "It's hard to tell from all the tiny pieces what it was supposed to be."

"Stop it," I exclaimed, trying to hide the smile that slid across my face.

"Okay," Darian said, holding his hands up in surrender. "I wasn't going to ask about the plate until you brought it up." He chuckled.

I looked down at the palms of my hands, picking at a tiny sliver of glass embedded in the skin.

I heard Darian shift uncomfortably in his chair and suck in a deep breath, as if he was about to speak.

"Ari, we need to talk," he said softly, stretching his arm across the table to take my hand in his.

I looked up to meet his gaze with a cold stare. "There's nothing to say."

"I think there is," Darian continued. "Ever since the night we kissed, I think we've both been dreading the day this is all going to come to an end and you're going to leave."

"I *have* to leave," I protested.

"Not alone."

My breath caught in my lungs and it felt like someone was slowly squeezing all the air out of me.

"I'm coming with you, Ari."

Dozens of excuses and protests rose to my lips but he silenced them by leaning forward and pressing his lips gently against mine. I didn't pull away.

"I don't want to know what it's like to lose another person I love."

My heart hammered in my chest, racing headlong into a feeling I thought I would never experience.

"What about finding your parents?" I whispered.

"Maybe one day I will find them but I'm not going to throw away my future searching for a past I'm never going to have again."

I flung my arms around Darian's neck, feeling his heart thudding against mine under his thin cotton shirt.

I had no idea what saying yes to him would look like or how everything would play out. I didn't know if the Rose was even real or if Draxon would keep his word.

The only thing I knew for sure was that Darian loved me. And that was enough.

Chapter 11

I woke with a start to feel the ship heaving beneath me, the waves crashing against the side of the ship, unlike the gentle swaying I had grown used to. I heard the rumble of thunder and the thrum of rain on the deck outside my room. A feeling of unease washed over me as I tossed my blankets to the side and made my way toward the door.

I opened it and a cold gust of wind blew under my thin cotton shirt. I wrapped my arms tightly around my body and ran out onto the deck as heavy raindrops pelted down on me.

There were no sailors in sight. *How were they all sleeping through this storm? Was there no one on lookout?*

The sky was dark and the moon was covered by dark, heavy storm clouds. A bolt of lightning snaked across the sky, illuminating the turbulent sea that frothed and foamed like a rabid dog.

Amid the howling wind, I heard the sound of loud, angry voices. Another shiver ran down my spine. My shirt clung to my body and rain water ran down the sides of my face. I began to run around the deck, trying to find the source of the voices. They grew louder as I approached the railing below the crows nest and I could make out the outline of two men struggling on the deck.

"Is everything okay?" I called out, wondering if they were trying to secure something to the deck.

They didn't appear to hear me and I still couldn't distinguish who they were because of the blinding rain. A wave crashed over the side of the ship, catching me off balance and I fell to the deck. Water sloshed around my feet and I quickly got up, my teeth beginning to chatter from the icy water.

My breath caught in the back of my throat when I saw one of the men shove the other up against the railing.

Pulse racing, I ran towards the men, dread filling in the pit of my stomach. "Stop!" I screamed, charging at the man who had begun to lift the other up over the edge of the ship. The only thing separating him from the merciless sea was his adversary's grip on his leg. At any moment, that man could be dropped into the ocean.

Using my full body weight, I tackled him, wrapping my arms around his waist, just as he let go of his flailing victim, dropping him into the merciless sea.

We both sprawled on the deck and I thrust my fist into the side of his face, trying to escape his grasp. Another bolt of lightning streaked across the sky as I looked into the face of my opponent.

"Darian," I gasped, shock causing me to freeze and stop struggling.

"Ari?" he whispered, releasing his grip on my arm and staring into my wide eyes.

"Who...?" I began, unable to form a coherent sentence. My heart dropped while I stared into Darian's stormy green eyes, the colour of the waves churning below us.

"Ari, I'm so sorry, I can explain, I—"

I got to my feet, tugging at my wet shirt which clung to my skin. "Somebody please help," I cried, panic beginning to set in.

I frantically scanned the deck, looking for another sailor or Captain Carter.

"Ari, stop, I need to tell you something," pleaded Darian, grabbing onto my wrist tightly and pulling me closer to him.

"Get your hands off of me right now," I spat out with clenched teeth. "There is a man fighting for his life in the water and you don't even care."

"Ari, he's not who you think he is, he—"

"Who is he, Darian?" I cried. "Who did you throw overboard?"

A lump formed in the back of my throat and I felt burning anger bubbling up inside of me.

"What is going on here?" came a strong voice behind me.

Darian immediately let go of my wrist and I whirled around to see Captain Carter's concerned face staring at the two of us. His grey hair was slick against the sides of his face and water dripped from his beard.

"What are you doing, Darian? You were supposed to be on night watch. The rest of the crew is trying to take down the sails and secure the cargo down in the hold," he explained.

"Captain," I said, choking back a sob. "There's a man in the water," I said, gesturing out towards the sea that was growing more boisterous by the minute.

His face grew pale and his eyes widened as he searched my gaze. He ran to the railing, searching the waves.

"Who is it?" he asked, his eyes never leaving the deadly waters that tossed the ship around like a child playing with a toy in a wash basin.

My eyes bored into Darian's as I waited for his answer.

"It's Gabriel."

A shudder rippled through my body as Captain Carter turned towards me and placed a gentle hand on my shoulder. His solemn eyes locked with mine and I could see the words forming on his breath before he opened his mouth.

"I'm sorry Ari… the storm is too rough. I can't risk the lives of any more of my crew members. We'll never be able to rescue him."

I recoiled from his touch and began to back away from him towards the railing. I could feel the salty spray on my face as the wind whipped my hair into my eyes.

"You're going to look me in the eyes and tell me that you are going to let one of your own men die? You're going to let an innocent man drown in this storm!" I exclaimed, my voice growing louder as I spoke.

"He was never part of the crew, Ari. We don't know anything about him. He's not who you think he is," said Darian, taking a step towards me.

My chest constricted and it was as if there was an iron fist wrapped around my throat, squeezing the breath from my lungs.

"Liar," I spat, eyes flashing. "You never trusted him from the beginning, Darian, because you only saw him as competition for my heart. You are the real liar," I accused. "You are the one who has been trying to charm me with your sweet talk. But let me tell you this," I said, jabbing a finger into Darian's chest, "you never had my heart and you never will."

I withdrew my hand and put one foot on the edge of the railing, wrapping my arms around it to try to keep my balance as the ship rode the rising waves.

"Ari, what are you doing?" shouted Captain Carter with alarm. "What's going on here?"

"Ask Darian," I said, struggling to get a foothold on the railing, slick with water. "He's the one who threw Gabriel overboard."

Captain Carter turned to Darian, eyes widening. A shout came from across the ship as one of the sailors ran around the corner, trying futilely to wring some of the water out of his shirt.

"Cap'n, we can't get the sails lowered 'cause the wind is blowin' so fiercely," he said, his breath coming out in short bursts of air.

Captain Carter looked between Darian and I as the rain pounded down around us.

"Ari, please, I need you to get down from there," he begged. "Don't do something you will regret."

"The only thing I will regret is letting Gabriel die," I said, pulling my other leg over the edge of the railing.

Sucking in a deep breath, I looked down at the raging sea, the foam reaching up to touch the tips of my toes.

"Ari!" cried Darian, rushing towards me with his arms outstretched.

I let go of the railing. My stomach plummeted to my feet as I crashed into the waves.

Icy water stung my skin like tiny pin pricks. I sucked in deep gulps of air as I sputtered and coughed up the water that burned the back of my throat and lungs. I thrashed frantically in the churning sea, searching for the top of Gabriel's head. The waves rose higher and higher, obscuring my vision.

I blinked rapidly as the rain continued to fall, streaming down the sides of my face. I could make out the sound of Darian's voice calling to me from the ship but I couldn't distinguish what he was saying.

"Gabriel!" I screamed, reaching out an arm and trying to push through the waves. My heart raced furiously in my chest. I had to find him. The only thing that mattered now was saving his life.

The sky lit up with a crackle as another bolt of lightning struck. Out of the corner of my eye, I saw the mast of the ship, with the sails half lowered, lean precariously to one side as the port side of the ship careened towards me.

"Gabriel!" I cried out again. My call was silenced as a wave swept over me, knocking me onto my back and pushing me under water.

This wasn't how I was going to die, I told myself. I had a journey to complete and this was not how my life was going to end. And this wasn't how Gabriel would die either, I assured myself.

I pushed myself to the surface, my lungs burning for air as I coughed and sputtered. I let myself be swept along by the waves, tired of fighting against them. I scanned the sea, desperately hoping and praying for any sign of Gabriel.

I rubbed my burning eyes and began to swim towards what appeared to be a white object, tossed about in the water. My arms cut through the water, stroke after stroke, but it seemed that the more I swam, the object was pushed further away.

Frustration welled up inside me and I stopped to tread water. *Could it be Gabriel? Was he even still alive? Or was it just his body, face down in the water as the waves crashed around him?*

My chest constricted and blood pounded in my ears. I couldn't help but feel responsible for what had happened tonight. I was the one who had led Gabriel to the ship and given him hope that he could have a future. I was the one who had caught feelings for Darian and encouraged his attention. I didn't know what had transpired tonight but I had a feeling that Darian's feelings of resentment and jealousy of Gabriel had gotten the best of him.

But to push him overboard? I could not bring myself to believe that Darian had done such a thing. And yet, I had seen him do it with my own eyes.

Appearances may be deceiving but a person's actions never lie.

Darian had led me to believe he was a good man, one with a broken past, but someone who truly loved me. But that love had led him to harm Gabriel, someone who I cared about.

And that was unforgivable.

Catching sight of the white object, riding the waves in the distance, I began to swim towards it again, adrenaline surging through my veins. I felt a small twinge in the pit of my stomach that told me it was Gabriel—dead or alive, I wasn't sure.

Taking a deep breath, I stretched out my hand to touch the cold, white shirt clinging to Gabriel's back. Grabbing him tightly by the arms, I slowly flipped him over onto his back, trying to keep his head above water as the waves washed over him.

I held my hand over his mouth, panic consuming me when I felt no breath. His chest was still and his cheeks had lost all colour. Realizing that there was nothing I could do for him while he was in the water, I tried to pull him onto my back so I could swim back towards the ship.

Gabriel was a dead weight that hung off of me as the waves tugged at him, desperately trying to pull him back into the sea with their icy hands.

I kicked and paddled hard, straining against the added weight and the internal pressure I had placed on myself to save him.

I was on this ship to save my parents, but I was beginning to wonder if there was another reason that I had found myself here.

Brushing these thoughts aside, I focused my gaze on the *Maryanne*. The ship that had looked so big and regal in the harbour looked like a tiny speck on the sea, at the mercy of the storm.

Who knew if we would be safer on the ship than in the water?

"Somebody help me!" I screamed as I neared the ship, desperately hoping there would be someone there to help me get Gabriel back on the ship.

The sail appeared to be lowered and I could see the sailors running back and forth across the deck with buckets.

Dread sank like an anchor in my heart, fearing that the ship was going to sink. I had come this far and I couldn't fail now.

"Help!" I screamed, my voice growing hoarse as the wind blew my words away.

"She's over here," I heard a voice call out.

"Ari, are you okay?" cried Darian, leaning over the railing as the sailor next to him threw down a rope.

I grabbed the end of it, struggling to slide Gabriel off of my back and wrap the rope around him.

"Pull him up and then throw the rope back down to me," I instructed. "He's not breathing. You have to save him." My voice rose as I spoke, on the verge of hysteria as they began to pull Gabriel up.

"We'll do everything we can for him," promised the sailor, but his face looked grim. Darian stared down at me as I hung on to the side of the ship, trying not to get swept back out into the water. His gaze flickered from me to Gabriel's lifeless body.

A dark shadow passed over him and the light seemed to vanish from his green eyes.

I had opened myself up to Darian. I had trusted him with the deepest, darkest parts of myself. I thought he had opened up to me too. But it seemed as if there was another side to him that was only now being brought to light. A darkness that crept among the shadows of his heart, lurking around the corner just waiting to be unleashed.

And I feared that once the darkness escaped its cage, it could never be locked away again.

Chapter 12

I collapsed on the deck as Darian and a few other sailors helped to pull me up over the side of the ship. The waves continued to slam against the sides, spraying salt water into the air. I sat on the deck, trying to still my trembling body and my chattering teeth. I wrapped my arms around my body, doing little to shield myself from the rain pelting down all around me.

Out of the corner of my eye, I saw Darian kneel down beside me, resting a hand on my shoulder. I flinched at his touch and pulled away.

"Get your hands off of me," I growled, locking eyes with him.

"Ari, please—"

"Don't speak to me," I said, scrambling to my feet. My legs wobbled and I stumbled as the world spun around me. Black spots danced before my eyes and one of the sailors reached out an arm to steady me.

"I need to see Gabriel," I choked out. "Where is he?"

"Cap'n brought him into his quarters out of the rain so he could check on him. You should get out of the rain too," he said, concern lining his sharp features.

I allowed the sailor to lead me across the deck towards the captain's quarters, leaving Darian standing alone on the deck. I could feel his eyes boring into the back of my head but I refused to turn around.

Memories of sitting beside him in the crow's nest, my head resting on his shoulder as we watched the stars, flashed through my mind. I let the thought linger for a split second too long and I felt a painful tug in my chest.

I had thought leaving Darian behind when I left the ship would be painful but now, I felt like my heart was being stabbed by a million tiny pin pricks at the sight of him.

My body felt numb and I didn't know how to feel anymore. I regretted ever letting myself feel something for Darian. I never wanted to feel this way again.

The sailor opened the door and I saw the Captain leaning over Gabriel's still body. I forced myself to walk to his bedside, my heart galloping in my chest.

"Gabriel," I whispered, falling to my knees and taking his ice cold hand in mine. His normally thick mop of dark curly hair was slick against the side of his head and his eyes were closed.

I traced the edge of his jaw with my finger and laid my head against his chest, desperately hoping to feel his chest rise and fall with breath.

His chest rose ever so slightly beneath me and I felt tears of relief prick the backs of my eyes. I had already lost one person I had loved tonight. I couldn't lose another.

"He's alive but his breathing is shallow," said Captain Carter solemnly. "The storm is only getting worse and if he doesn't get proper medical attention soon….." His voice trailed off and I felt my heart sink. I tried to swallow around the giant lump that had formed in my throat.

No. No. I repeated this over and over in my head, unable to speak audibly but inside, I was screaming. This was not how things were supposed to go. We were supposed to arrive safely in port at Destin tomorrow. I would get off the ship alone and find the Red Rose.

Hitting a storm and Darian throwing Gabriel overboard was not part of that plan. I wanted to wake up, safe and warm in my bed at the palace and have all of this just be one horrible dream.

But this was real life and there was nothing I could do to change it. I was a puppet on a string in some maniac's cruel little game and there was no way to escape. No matter how hard I tried to escape the puppeteer's grasp, the harder he held on to me.

"Ari, you need to rest," said Captain Carter, his brow furrowing with worry.

"No," I said, barely audible.

"You're exhausted and have been through a lot. Let us deal with Gabriel."

"No," I repeated, my voice growing stronger and louder. "I can't rest at a time like this! I need to talk to Darian," I said, decisively. "He can not get away with this."

I stood up at Gabriel's bedside, casting one last look at his deathly pale face.

"Ari, please," begged Captain Carter. He did not try to stop me as I brushed past him and out the door. My mind was made up. Darian would pay for this.

I was met with a gust of wind and pelted with icy rain. "Darian!" I screamed, searching the deck of ragged sailors.

I watched him duck behind two of the sailors and disappear around the corner. I knew where he was headed. *Coward.*

I raced across the deck, my hair blowing into my eyes and mouth but I didn't care. All that mattered was finding Darian.

I rounded the corner to see him scrambling up the ladder to the crow's nest. "Darian!" I called, beginning to scramble up the ladder after him.

He paused on the ladder, turning around to look down at me. "What are you doing, Ari?"

"I need to talk to you!"

"There's nothing to talk about," he said. "You won't believe me anyways. Why don't you go back to Gabriel?" he spat bitterly. There was no anger in his eyes, only pain and sadness.

"You owe me an explanation," I said.

"I don't owe you anything." He turned back around and climbed into the crow's nest.

Frustration welled up inside of me and I made my way up the rest of the ladder and climbed up onto the lookout beside him.

"What do you have against Gabriel? Why did you throw him overboard?" I grabbed onto his arms and began shaking him, trying to understand what had happened to the boy I thought I had loved.

"Gabriel is dying and it's all your fault! He's barely breathing! All he wanted was a fresh start and a life away from the streets," I said, my voice breaking.

"Is that what he told you?" said Darian, a dark look passing over his face. "I don't know who Gabriel is but I don't trust him. How do you know he's telling the truth?"

I paused, letting his words sink in. A bolt of lightning cracked above our heads, dangerously close.

"Darian, I don't know much about him but I still trust him more than you right now. I thought I knew who you were but the boy I knew would never have tried to kill an innocent man." I stared at him as one tear and then another slid down his cheeks.

"I loved you, Darian."

His throat bobbed and he swiped at his cheeks, his tears mixing with the rain.

"I was trying to protect you, Ari. I love you and nothing is going to change that."

"I don't need you to protect me. Like you said, you don't owe me anything. We're nothing more than two people whose paths crossed for a short time. And I don't expect them to cross again."

"Please don't do this," pleaded Darian, coming up to me and resting a hand on the side of my face.

I froze, looking into his glassy, green eyes. He leaned forward and pressed his lips against mine. For a split second, I forgot he was supposed to be my enemy and that I had to let him go. For a minute, I imagined what things would be like if we had met back home under completely different circumstances. And in that moment, I wanted to kiss him back, to make him mine forever.

I pulled away. "Goodbye Darian."

Another bolt of lightning flashed across the sky as I turned my back on him for the last time. I began to climb back down the ladder, my hands slipping on the wood, slick with water.

I felt a sudden searing pain in my left arm, like fire running through my veins, burning me from the inside out. I hissed with pain, letting go of the ladder with one hand to clutch my arm.

Darian took a step towards me, concern replacing the sadness in his eyes.

My head began to spin as black spots speckled my vision. I felt my grip on the rung of the ladder slipping as I struggled to push through the pain.

"Ari, take my hand," said Darian, reaching out his arm towards me.

I stared up at him, fighting against the fire in my veins and the pain in my heart. A jabbing pain, sharper than before shot up my arm and I let go of the rung of the ladder. Darian's face grew blurry and I felt myself teetering on the edge of the ladder before I felt myself falling.

The sounds of the rain, the crashing waves and the shouting voices of the sailors faded as blood pounded in my ears. Then, there was only darkness.

Chapter 13

My eyelids were heavy like lead weights as I attempted to open them. They fluttered open briefly but then I closed them as the world spun around me. I felt chilled and I burrowed deeper under the soft blankets which smelled faintly of honey and herbs. I thought I heard voices but they were quiet and sounded far off. My left arm burned and throbbed but exhaustion overwhelmed me and I was too tired to care. I felt my body succumb to sleep again as my surroundings faded into a dream.

The sound of battle cries and clanging swords rang in the air around me. Soldiers dressed in palace uniforms were sprawled on the cold stone floor of the palace, dark pools of blood surrounding them.

I heard Draxon's evil cackle in my ear and then his face appeared. He had an evil sneer on his face that could not be erased.

Out of the corner of my eye I saw my parents chained together with two guards holding blades to their necks.

"This is what happens to those who betray me," said Draxon, his eyes glittering with satisfaction.

He nudged the corpse at his feet so the face was turned towards me. A lock of dark curly hair fell to the side, revealing Gabriel's pale, bloodied face. I dropped to my knees beside him, my heart catching in my throat as I saw that his chest was still, no longer rising and falling with each breath.

I awoke again with a jolt, heart racing and covered in a cold sweat. The searing pain in my arm was even stronger than before. I was still tired but the dizziness had subsided. I didn't trust myself to sit up yet, so I just laid there and tried to calm the building terror within me.

Questions filled my mind, making me feel anxious and discontent. *What had Draxon done to my parents? Where was Gabriel? Was he all right? What did my dream mean? Was it just a dream, or a vision, destined to come true?*

My eyes began to focus on my surroundings and I realized I was no longer on board the *Maryanne*. I did not recognize anything and I no longer felt the swaying of the ship or the familiar sound of water splashing against the sides I had grown accustomed to.

So where was I? Where was everyone else? Had I been abducted? I heard voices and I turned to see where they were coming from. The door to the small room I was occupying opened and a small, wizened old woman entered, followed by Captain Carter and Gabriel.

"Ari," Gabriel exclaimed as he ran to my side and clasped my cold, pale hand in his. I looked him in the eyes and I could see worry etched into the lines of his face.

"Now, now, give the girl some space. That's a boy," chided the old woman.

He reluctantly let go of my hand and backed away, giving me space as the woman had instructed.

"I'm Daphne," she said with a kind smile. "How are you feeling?"

"Much better," I replied. "Most of the dizziness and aching is gone now."

"Mmm," she murmured to herself. "Hey Carter, would you please fetch me that cup over there." She pointed to a small table in the far corner by the door. "Yes, that's the one," she said as he retrieved the cup. He handed it to her and she brought the cup to my lips. "Now I want you to drink this," she whispered. "It'll make you feel just like new."

I tentatively opened my mouth and allowed her to pour the hot, steaming liquid down my throat. I almost choked on the first sip. It was bitter but it didn't taste too bad. Like fruit with a gingery flavour to it. The tangy liquid made my chest feel warm and fuzzy inside.

When I finished, I turned to face Captain Carter. "What happened? Where am I?"

"Well," he began, sucking in a deep breath. "I managed to get the ship close enough to shore that we were able to anchor down until the storm was over. It was a miracle for sure. If not for that, we wouldn't be here right now." It was a solemn thought.

"And here is…?"

"Destin. You've been in and out of unconsciousness for four days. You had a high fever and we weren't sure if you were going to make it."

I couldn't believe it. For almost a week, I had been sick and I didn't remember a single thing.

"What was wrong with me?" I asked Daphne. I vaguely remembered a storm and something happening between Darian and Gabriel, although I couldn't remember what. I recalled feeling tired and confused before, but enough to be sick for days? It seemed crazy and impossible.

"I'm not sure, dear. You would stir and I would give you herbal teas and bathe your face with a damp cloth but you would never fully awaken." Her brow furrowed in intent concentration. "I tried using some of my strongest medicines but it appears that there must be an even stronger power at work within you."

"What?" *What was she talking about? What did she mean by a strong power working in me?*

"Well, I did notice something rather odd," she said, looking at me with an unreadable expression on her face. "A strange mark on your left arm."

My heart stopped beating for a split second as I protectively grabbed onto the sleeve of my nightgown which Daphne must have put on me. I rolled up the sleeve of my gown to reveal a red mark in the shape of a rose that sprawled across my skin.

"You mean this?" I asked, watching as the woman's eyes widened with wonder. "I've had this my whole life. My parents said it's a birthmark," I explained.

Gabriel moved closer to my bed and Captain Carter looked at me, opening his mouth as if he was going to speak and then closing it.

"Doesn't look like any birthmark I've ever seen before," said Daphne, reaching out a warm hand to run her finger along the rose.

"I was told recently by someone that this mark relates to an ancient legend about a mythical flower," I explained, choosing my words with caution.

The three gathered around me in the small room listened intently to my every word.

"He said it was a marker that allowed me to access this magical flower and no one else can. Honestly, I don't trust him. It's probably all just a made up story," I said, brushing my own words away with a wave of my hand.

I looked at Daphne whose eyes were wide and glittered with excitement. "The Red Rose....." she whispered, as if she could scarcely believe it.

Shivers ran down my spine at her words. "What do you know about the Red Rose," I asked her, leaning forward in bed.

"The Red Rose is an Oberian legend stating that there is a magical flower that has power to do almost anything the human mind can dream up, even power to control life and death itself. Since its powers are so strong, there is a *Keeper*, someone who is appointed every century to care for the flower and who has access to it. No one except for the *Keeper* can retrieve the Rose."

"How is the *Keeper* chosen?" interrupted Gabriel, appearing uneasy about the whole idea.

"I don't know," said Daphne with a casual shrug of her shoulders. "Magic rarely has a logical explanation, dear."

I felt a tingling sensation in my arm, different from the burning pain I had experienced before.

"So you think I'm the *Keeper* of the Rose?" I asked, incredulously.

Daphne only smiled, not offering any further explanation.

Gabriel held his hands up in the air, unable to process what was said. "What does all of this mean?" he asked, looking at the old woman who had stood, ready to leave the room.

"I think that is a question only Ari can answer," she replied.

I began to protest, my mind whirling with my own questions for the woman. She seemed to know more about this than anyone I had spoken to.

Daphne nodded to Captain Carter to follow her out of the room. I watched their retreating backs as they shut the door behind them, leaving me alone with Gabriel.

The boy I thought I had lost the night of the storm. Memories and tumultuous emotions overwhelmed me as I remembered the weight of Gabriel's lifeless body in my arms.

"You're alive," I said, forcing a laugh to lighten the mood. I reached out an arm to touch his cheek, to feel his warm breath on my hand, as if making sure he was really there.

"So are you," he said with an awkward chuckle.

There was silence as we both gazed into each other's eyes, both haunted by the other's close encounter with death. I was the first to look away.

"Where is....?" I let the unfinished question hang in the air, unable to bring myself to say *his* name.

I felt Gabriel tense beside me and he hesitated before speaking. "*He* is with the other sailors at the inn, waiting for the repairs to be finished on the ship. Due to the storm and our rough history with each other, he is being given a free pass this time. No charges are being held against him since there is no one to prove who started the fight," explained Gabriel through gritted teeth.

I felt my chest tighten at his words. Darian deserved to be punished for what he had done. It was not right for him to get away with this. But another part of me felt secretly relieved. I didn't know if I could bear the thought of him being sent to prison.

"What happened between you two?" I asked, prodding at the still fresh wound I knew Gabriel covered just below the surface.

"Ari," said Gabriel, lowering his voice to a whisper, "I didn't want to tell you this because I honestly wanted to believe the best in Darian too." His eyes held no anger of malice in them, only sincerity.

"Please tell me," I begged. "I need to know the truth."

"How much does Darian know about the Rose?"

My mind flickered to our conversation that night that now felt so long ago in the crow's nest when we had kissed. I had told him about Draxon holding my family hostage and how he wanted me to find the Red Rose. I had shown him the mark on my arm.

"Everything," I said, an uneasy feeling forming in the pit of my stomach. More than even Gabriel knew.

Gabriel shook his head and I could tell that whatever his suspicions were, they had been confirmed.

"What is it?" I asked, bracing myself for what he was going to say next.

"Darian knows who you are," he said, letting the words fall from his lips. "He knows you are the *Keeper* and that you can access the power of the Red Rose."

Dread pooled inside of me and I grabbed Gabriel's hand in my clammy, sweaty one.

"He wants the Rose, Ari. He wants it for himself."

I felt a sharp pain in my chest, as if someone had driven me through with a sword. That might have been less painful than this.

"What are you talking about, Gabriel? Why would he want the Red Rose? He would never use me like this," I exclaimed, willing myself to believe my own words. No matter what Darian had done to Gabriel, he would never betray me like this.

"I don't believe you," I said, disbelief filling my mind.

Gabriel's face was grim and I could tell it hurt him to tell me this. *Why would he make this up?*

"I know this is hard to believe, Ari, but what I'm saying is the truth. I don't know why he would do this but it's easy to guess. Who wouldn't want that kind of power?"

My mind ran to all the things Darian had revealed to me about his past, about wanting to find his parents and have the life he had only ever dreamed of having. The Red Rose would allow him to have his dream and so much more.

I was only one small sacrifice he had to make to get it. An easy trade in his mind, clearly. I could see him now, see all his smiles, his kisses, his care and concern for me was all a lie, used to gain my trust and information about the Rose. Maybe it had been real at first, before he knew who I was. But none of that mattered now.

I felt dirty, cheated and exposed. I had let Darian see the parts of my heart I had never let anyone see before. I had trusted him with my story and he had never cared. He only wanted me for what I could give him.

I expected to feel sadness, to feel tears pouring down my cheeks but instead, I felt a dull ache in my chest and a hollowness unlike anything I had ever felt before.

I was a pawn in Draxon's game and now I had been used as a pawn in Darian's too. Never again would I let myself fall so easily for someone.

"I have to go," I said abruptly, pushing my blankets to the side and leaping out of bed.

Gabriel fell back, caught off guard by my sudden insistence. "What are you talking about? Where are you going? You need to rest," he said, grabbing my arm to pull me back towards the bed.

I jerked away from him and he flinched, as if he thought I was going to hit him. "I'm tired of resting. I'm tired of sitting around and letting myself be a pawn in everyone else's game. It's time I did what I came here to do," I said firmly.

I scrambled around the tiny room, searching for my clothes and my backpack. I found them sitting on a small table beside a stack of clean towels. I grabbed my tattered shirt and pants and hurriedly began to dress myself, not caring that Gabriel was in the room.

"Ari. you're acting crazy right now," he said, having the decency to turn and face the wall as I changed. "You're not going out to look for the Rose by yourself after you just survived a shipwreck."

"I don't have a choice," I said with frustration, pulling my shirt over my head. "My parents' lives are hanging in the balance and I will not be the cause of their death."

"You won't be helping them by going and getting yourself killed," snapped Gabriel, turning back around to face me as I slipped my feet into my boots and knelt to tie the laces.

"I will do whatever it takes to save them or else die trying," I said, hearing the fire in my own voice.

Gabriel let out an exasperated sigh as I swung my backpack over my shoulder and made a beeline for the door. "If you insist on going, then you're not going alone," he called after me.

I ignored him, charging out the bedroom door and past Daphne and Carter who looked at me with alarm.

"What is that girl doing out of bed?" exclaimed Daphne with alarm. She set her cup of tea on the counter with a clatter and turned to Gabriel who had followed me out into the kitchen.

"Don't ask questions," he said, coming to my defense. "I'll look out for her."

Daphne and Carter both began to protest but I silenced them with a determined look that said, "I'm going and there is nothing you can do about it."

Knowing better than to argue with me, they both fell silent, watching Gabriel and I disappear out the door of the tiny log house without another word.

"You better not slow me down," I said, squinting as we stepped into the sunlight. The brightness made my eyes water after being in the dark bedroom for so many days.

"I won't," said Gabriel with a chuckle. "We'll see if you can keep up with me," he quipped, breaking into fast, long strides with his tall, gangly legs. "I outrun folks like you on the streets for a livin' remember?"

I smirked. "You didn't outrun me."

Gabriel conceded, his face flushing. "How could I forget?"

I felt a tiny flutter in my stomach, remembering how I had first met him on the streets. So much had happened in such a short time and yet, it felt like that moment in the wharf had happened in another lifetime. And yet here we were, *together*.

By some random chance of fate, I was the girl who had been chosen to be the *Keeper* of some magical flower, setting in motion a turn of events I never could have imagined in my worst nightmare— and in some ways, my wildest dreams.

Some might say I was a puppet on a string, a pawn in a game. I had believed it and maybe there was some truth to it. But I was tired of being the victim, manipulated by everyone around me.

I was finally taking the situation into my own hands, the fate of my parents and my country. And no one—not Darian, not Draxon, not even fate itself— was going to stand in my way.

Chapter 14

The town of Destin was small, nestled on the edge of the ocean, surrounded by a sprawling coastline. Gabriel and I set out along a winding dirt road that went through the center of town and into the forest that stretched for miles on the opposite side of the island.

"It will probably take two days to get across the island," Gabriel remarked, studying the weathered map I held in my hands. I was lucky my things had survived the storm.

I suppressed a heavy sigh, running a tired hand through my tangled hair. It had been almost two weeks since I left Aurora and my family behind and I was more than ready to return. The days and weeks seemed to blend together, filled with fear and worry about what awaited me when I reached my home. Even if we did somehow manage to defeat Draxon and save my parents, it would only be a matter of time until he came back to seek his revenge.

And I could not let that happen. Even if it meant killing Draxon myself. We might have the same blood running through our veins but he was no blood of mine.

As if reading my hopeless thoughts, Gabriel reached out to lay a comforting hand on my shoulder. "It's going to be okay. You don't have to do this alone."

Frustration bubbled up inside of me as I looked up into his face, the familiar twinkle in his eyes replaced with a deep ache I couldn't understand.

"Yes, I do," I replied, shaking my head. "You might be able to accompany me now until we get the Rose, but after that, I'm going home alone. If Draxon sees you, he *will* kill you." At this point, it was one of the only things I could be certain of. Anyone who was an ally of mine was his enemy. I couldn't be responsible for the death of someone else I cared about.

"What about you?" asked Gabriel, a dark shadow passing over him. "Do you really think Draxon is going to let you live? Do you think he is going to go peacefully once he has the Rose? Is that all he wants?"

No. My family would always be a threat to him, one step between him and the crown he had always wanted. But Gabriel didn't know that. And he couldn't find out.

"I'll figure it out on my own," I said firmly, clenching my jaw.

Gabriel fell silent, his pace quickened to keep up with me. He made no effort to reply. This conversation was over.

I focused on the ground as I walked, following the ruts in the dirt from the carts, transporting cargo to and from the harbour. The bustling of the town faded away as we followed the road from Destin into the long stretch of country that laid between me and the Red Rose.

"I know you want to help me," I said suddenly, breaking the silence between us. "But what are you gaining from this?"

"What do you mean?" asked Gabriel defensively, casting me a sidelong glance.

"I mean that the *Maryanne* was your second chance, an opportunity to have a job and a better life. Why would you want to come with me when I offer no guarantees of any kind?"

Gabriel scoffed. "You call travelling around on a ship from port to port, never settling down or having a family of your own a *better life*?"

I shrugged, caught off guard by his reaction.

"I'm not helping you for what I can get out of this," Gabriel said, avoiding my gaze and looking down at his dusty boots.

"I know," I said, "but I just want you to know that you don't owe me anything. Come with me if you want but I will not ask you to stay. You're free to leave whenever you want."

Gabriel's face drained of colour and a solemn expression came over him.

"What's wrong?" I pressed, a sinking feeling filling the pit of my stomach.

"Nothing," he muttered.

Wordlessly, I reached out and grabbed his hand in mine. His shoulders immediately tensed and I thought he was going to pull away. Instead, I felt his fingers interlace with mine and I gave his hand a reassuring squeeze.

Darian might have betrayed me but Gabriel would never walk away.

"My mama said almost those exact same words to my father the night he left us," murmured Gabriel, a dark look entering his hazel eyes.

I looked at him with shock, unsure whether to say something or wait for him to continue.

"I'm sor—"

"Don't be sorry. My father was not a good man. I've been thieving on the streets since I was five years old so I could buy medicine for my ma. But my father would beat me if I didn't give him the money. He would spend all our savings on liquor."

My stomach lurched at his words and I felt a hollow ache in my chest for this man who had grown up in such poverty and hardship. Guilt pricked my conscience as I thought about how I had never gone a day in my life without food on the table or a hug and kiss goodnight from both my parents. Gabriel had never had that.

"My ma was always weak and most days could hardly get out of bed. But she did her best to care for me in whatever way she could. When my father would get in one of his stupors, she would take me outside to the woodshed and we would sit in there, wrapped in blankets and she would tell me stories until I fell asleep." Gabriel's eyes wavered with unshed tears and his hand felt clammy and cold in mine.

"You don't have to tell me all of this if you don't want to," I offered, not wanting him to feel obligated to continue.

"I want to," he said firmly. "I will *not* become my father. That's why I need to do this."

"That's why you need to come with me?" I asked, slightly confused.

He didn't answer my question, instead, choosing to continue on with his story.

"The night my father left, he was in a rage, throwing whatever was in sight. I was huddled in the corner, wrapped in blankets, terrified that my father was going to kill Ma."

A faraway look entered his eyes as he relived the horrors of that night. "I'll never forget how my ma got out of bed and looked my father in the eye and told him, 'You have not been a husband to me or a father to our son. I could choose to hold it against you, make you stay and become the man I always thought you were. But I've realized that will never happen. You don't owe us anything. The door has been open since the day you picked up that first bottle of liquor. You're free to leave whenever you want. I won't ask you to stay.'"

Shivers ran down my spine and it was as if I was huddled beside him on the floor, watching the scene transpire.

"I remember my father raising his fists, his face red and the vein in his neck bulging so much I thought it was going to explode. There was no fear in my ma's eyes. He looked at her and then to me, huddled in the corner. Then, he lowered his arms and walked out the door and never looked back. That was the last time I ever saw him."

I let out a deep breath of relief, but as I looked at Gabriel, I knew his father would always be a ghost that haunted his past that he could never quite be rid of. And his greatest fear was that he would become him.

"My ma died less than a year later, when I was nine years old. So I was left on the streets, staying in country folks' barns, stealing to survive. Until the day you met me," he said, a faint teasing glimmer returning to his eyes.

"I had no idea, Gabriel. I can't even begin to imagine what that must have been like for you," I said.

"I don't expect a girl who has lived a life of luxury to understand," he replied.

"What do you mean?" I asked, feeling the blood drain from my face. I jerked my hand out of his grasp. *Did he know who I was?*

His face paled too and he looked away. "Anyone with eyes can tell you aren't from a poor family."

I looked down at my dirty, sweat stained clothes, the ends of my shirt tattered and worn.

"The day I met you at the wharf," he explained, "when I tried to steal from you. I could tell you weren't from a poor family or else I wouldn't have."

After I had listened to his story and tried to comfort him, he responded by telling me that he didn't expect me to understand? Anger welled up inside of me. I might not have come from a life of poverty but I still understood hardship and loss.

I walked faster, trying to put some space between us.

"Ari, I'm sorry, I didn't mean it like that," he protested.

"It's okay, I understand. Since I didn't grow up in poverty there is no way I could possibly have experienced any type of hardship in my life."

"No!" exclaimed Gabriel. "I'm sorry, I don't know what I was thinking. I know you've been through a lot too."

"I know we are very different, Gabriel, but I'm trying to understand. You shared your story with me and I listened and then you just turned on me. How am I supposed to react?"

Gabriel opened his mouth to reply but quickly closed it, as if thinking better of his retort. Frustration filled me and I found myself thinking about how much easier it would have been for me to have gone on this journey alone, never letting myself get close to people or build friendships. Because this was just so much more complicated. I had allowed myself to get hurt by people I had come to care about and soon I would have to leave them behind.

Being a princess, I had been sheltered from the outside world. My only friends were the children of staff who worked at the palace. But even then, I had always known my title and my crown were a barrier between us and ultimately, my kingdom was where my allegiance laid.

And my loyalty was still to my country. Something had shifted inside of me over this journey though. I had gotten to experience life, even for a brief time, as Ari. No crown, no title, no wealth or kingdom. I was just *me*.

It was freeing and sometimes, I wished I didn't have those responsibilities or burdens. *But who would I be without them?*

I didn't know. And I wasn't sure I wanted to.

If Draxon won and I still lived at the end of it, I would be banished from the kingdom, free to live a normal life without ties to the crown.

In the end, things would go back to the way they were and I would continue to be Her Royal Highness, Princess Arianna Alexandra Quintis, heir of the Oberian crown.

This was my life. I had been born into a world with a crown waiting for me and I would die and leave a throne behind for one of my heirs. Wishing for anything different was futile.

Chapter 15

The sun was a low, fiery, orange ball on the horizon, its last faint rays of light peeking through the boughs of the trees lining the narrow path. I rolled my shoulders back, trying to ignore the ache in my back from carrying my bag.

"We're going to need to find somewhere to stay for the night," I said.

Gabriel smirked. "We're in the middle of nowhere," he said with a chuckle. "Good luck with that. I think we're going to be sleeping under the stars tonight."

My stomach sank at the thought. I had one small blanket, an empty canteen, the map and compass but no food or other supplies. There was no way I was sleeping outside on the cold, wet ground in the middle of a forest with who knew what kinds of wild animals.

"Let's keep walking. There's got to be something around here," I persisted.

"Whatever you say," teased Gabriel.

We walked a few more miles in silence, listening to the crackle of leaves underfoot, the skittering of squirrels running in the trees above us and the faint rustle of wind as a cool breeze blew around us.

Up ahead the trees began to thin out and the path began to widen, beginning to give the appearance of a dirt road. There were no wagon tracks or hoof prints so I doubted anyone ever traveled this way. We rounded a bend in the road and I could make out a small wooden building that looked like it was leaning precariously to one side.

"Look," I shouted, pointing at the rickety building up ahead.

"Ari, I doubt there's anyone there. It looks abandoned."

Ignoring his comment and remaining hopeful, we neared the small building that looked like a house. The wood was cracked and rotting and there was a sign beside the door which read *"Thalia's Tavern."*

"Let's take a look inside," I urged.

Gabriel looked skeptical but reluctantly followed me.

The place was dimly lit and smelled musty. There were a few empty tables and chairs scattered around the room and a counter lined with bottles of liquor. The place was eerily quiet.

"I don't like the looks of this, Ari," warned Gabriel.

"Well, if there's no one here, it would be better to sleep inside than in the middle of the woods." I slung my backpack off of my shoulders and set it down on a nearby chair. A cloud of dust flew into the air, sending me into a coughing fit.

"Can I help you?" came a gravelly voice, causing my heart to leap out of my chest.

I whirled around to see a short, hunched, old woman, with hundreds of deep creases in her skin.

"We're very sorry to intrude. We'll be leaving now," said Gabriel apologetically, grabbing my arm to lead me back outside.

"No, stay and have some rum," replied the woman, her voice creaking like a door on rusty hinges.

Gabriel and I exchanged glances, not sure what to do.

"I rarely have visitors in these parts, especially not a young couple like you two," she continued, beckoning us towards the counter.

"Oh, we're not a couple," I explained, feeling the heat rise up into my face at her assumption.

I could sense Gabriel shifting uncomfortably beside me and he cleared his throat loudly. I ignored him and followed the lady over to the counter, taking a seat on one of the stools.

"I'm Thalia," she said, "but of course, you already knew that from the sign outside." She chuckled but it sounded unnatural, like a deep, guttural sound coming from her throat. She busied herself grabbing two glasses from the cabinet behind her and retrieved a pitcher of rum.

"What brings you to these parts?" asked the woman, inquisitively, casting a sidelong glance at Gabriel who had finally come and taken a seat beside me.

"We came on a ship to Destin and are touring the countryside," I lied, trying to avoid eye contact with the woman who looked like she was scrutinizing me.

"We don't get many travellers who wander this way," she replied, raising an eyebrow pointedly in my direction.

I shifted uncomfortably, hoping for a change in subject.

"I do like the business though," she chuckled. "These perfectly good bottles of liquor are just sitting here collecting dust."

I smiled, relaxing my shoulders and unclasping my hands. Thalia pushed two glasses of rum across the counter towards Gabriel and I.

"Drink up," she said.

Parched from the day's travels since our water had long since run out, I brought the cool glass to my lips and took a large swig, letting the sweet liquid trickle down my throat.

I heard Gabriel's hearty laugh beside me and I quickly turned to face him. "What are you laughing at?" I asked.

"You," he replied coyly. "I never thought I would see the day that you would drink rum."

"I'm thirsty," I complained. "Besides, you think girls can't drink liquor?"

"I'm not saying that," he said, his eyes glittering gleefully. "I just didn't expect it from you."

A giggle escaped my lips and I watched him over the rim of my cup as I took another swig, continuing to let the liquid pour down my throat until there was none left. I set the glass down on the table with a resounding clunk, listening to the sound of Gabriel's laughter ringing in the empty room. I began to laugh uncontrollably, feeling the rum swishing around in my belly, creating a warm feeling inside of me.

Out of the corner of my eye I saw Thalia watching us with a smirk on her face. She reached over the counter to grab my glass, refilling it with more rum.

"You know, you're different than I thought you would be," said Gabriel, his laughter subsiding. He studied me intently, as if trying to read my emotions.

My stomach did a flip-flop. "What did you expect me to be like?"

"Definitely not the kind of girl who would board a cargo ship of men and hold her own, or a girl who would chug a glass of rum."

I laughed, leaning forward and sliding my elbow along the counter and resting my cheek in my hand. "Well, I would hate to be predictable."

"I like unpredictable," said Gabriel with a grin.

He leaned forward ever so slightly and my breath caught in my throat. I felt his warm breath on my face.

"Cheers," he said, holding up his glass with an infuriating twinkle in his eyes.

I cursed inwardly, giving him a hard punch in the gut. His rum sloshed out of his glass and ran down his shirt.

"Hey!" he exclaimed in mock anger.

I grabbed my own glass and held it up. "Cheers," I said, devilishly, clinking my glass against his.

I took a sip, never taking my eyes off of Gabriel. His clothes clung to his body from sweat and he had a streak of dirt running down the left side of his jaw. The rum stain on his shirt added to his disheveled appearance and I was sure I didn't look much better. But somehow, none of that mattered.

I was an ocean away sitting in a bar with a boy I had only known for a few weeks. I had been betrayed once but I wouldn't let that happen again. I wondered what I had seen in Darian when Gabriel had been in front of me the whole time.

He had his past and I had mine but he had proved that he wasn't going anywhere.

As I drained the rest of my glass of rum, I saw Thalia emerge from a door behind the counter.

"Do you folks have a place to stay tonight? I know it's not much, but I have an extra room upstairs you could stay in. Sometimes I rent it out to guests but it hasn't been used in years."

"Thank you so much for the offer but we should probably get going," I said, looking to Gabriel for confirmation. "And we have no way to pay you." I pulled two gold coins from my pocket and placed them on the counter.

"That's all I have," I explained. "Take that for the rum." I stood up but immediately felt my body begin to sway and my knees went weak.

Gabriel grabbed onto my arms and helped me sit back down on the stool.

"I think your girl had a little too much to drink," said Thalia, donning her familiar smirk.

I felt my face heat up with embarrassment as Gabriel and Thalia laughed.

"Don't worry about the cost. The room is yours," she said, giving Gabriel a suggestive wink.

"It's not like that," I protested. The woman did not seem to believe me, yet again.

Before I could resist, Gabriel scooped me up in his arms and began to carry me towards the stairs on the opposite side of the bar.

I giggled, laying my head back against Gabriel's shoulders, letting him carry me up the stairs. When we reached the top, there was a single door which swung open on creaky hinges. The room was dim as night had fallen outside the window on the far side of the room. There was a small bed that did not look like it was made for two. The air smelled musty but the sheets looked clean, as if Thalia had been expecting us.

"This looks cozy," said Gabriel, approaching the bed and laying me down gently.

"I'm sorry for making you carry me," I said, looking up at him, apologetically.

"Don't be," he said with a wink.

I blushed, not sure how to respond to his remark.

Gabriel cast another glance around the small room, wandering over to a beige armchair in the corner. "You can take the bed," he offered. "I'll sleep here," he said, gesturing to the chair.

"No!" I exclaimed adamantly. "I'm not letting you sleep there. That doesn't look comfortable at all."

I stifled a giggle as Gabriel sat down in the chair, a cloud of dust enveloping him and sending him into a coughing fit.

I patted the bed beside me. He shifted in the chair, looking unsure as to whether or not he should accept my offer.

After a moment of hesitation, he stood up and walked over to the bed and perched on the edge beside me.

"I guess we should head to bed now if you want to leave early tomorrow," said Gabriel.

"Yes," I agreed. I was exhausted from the day's travels and my body ached.

Gabriel arched his back as he slowly pulled his shirt over his head, the muscles in his arms rippling. He tossed the stained piece of clothing on the floor and flopped on his back onto the bed. I laid down beside him, trying not to let my body brush against his.

I considered going and sleeping in the chair myself but I knew Gabriel would never let me. I doubted I would sleep either way.

I felt Gabriel's eyes on me and I turned to face him. My heart raced wildly in my chest, like a horse galloping across a pasture, preparing to jump a fence. I was close to the line but I would not cross it. There was no use getting my heart even more tangled up in the web I had spun for myself.

"Why you?" murmured Gabriel.

"What do you mean?" I asked, not sure where he was going with this.

"Why did Draxon have to choose you?"

My mind flashed back to our conversation in my room on the ship when I told him about the mark on my arm and how I was the only one who could access the Rose.

"I already told you," I said.

Gabriel looked at me with glassy eyes and I knew he wasn't talking about me going to find the Rose. I saw a flicker of emotion cross his face. For a split second, I saw regret in his eyes.

Possibly regret that he had chosen to come with me. Regret that he was falling in love. I wasn't sure.

But I had my own regrets. Regret that I had pushed Gabriel away and chosen Darian over him. Regret that I had closed myself off to Gabriel when all he wanted was for me to let him in.

"What are you thinking about in that pretty head of yours?" asked Gabriel, reaching out a hand to brush a strand of blonde hair off of my forehead.

A thousand words bubbled up inside of me, things I wished I could tell him. My breath caught in my throat as I fought between my heart and my brain, not sure what the right thing to do was.

"You mostly," I whispered.

I saw the questions in his eyes and the tiniest glimmer of hope.

"And how I wish I had let you kiss me that night on the ship." I bit my lip, letting the words hang in the air between us.

He brought his head closer to mine. "I wish you had let me too."

Leaning in, our lips met and I felt butterflies dance in my stomach. The kiss was sweet but ended too soon.

"Goodnight Ari," he said.

"Goodnight," I whispered back. I let my eyelids flutter closed as a wave of tiredness swept over me.

And I found myself wishing I could fall asleep next to Gabriel every night and that I would never have to say goodbye to him. Because I didn't know if when the time came, I would be able to let him go.

Chapter 16

I awoke to gentle sunlight cascading in through the partially open window. I blinked against the brightness, trying to remember where I was. My heart skipped a beat as I realized I was lying with my head against Gabriel's chest, his hand nestled in my hair.

Warmth filled me as I thought about our kiss last night and how it had felt to fall asleep next to him.

"Good morning," I said, snuggling deeper into Gabriel's arms. He stirred and opened his eyes. A grin slid across his face when he saw me next to him.

"I could get used to this," he said.

"Me too," I whispered. I felt as if something had changed between us last night and whatever it was, I didn't want it to end.

"I think we overslept," commented Gabriel, eyeing the bright sunshine that cast shadows on the walls.

I sat upright, remembering how far we still had to travel today if we wanted to reach the Rose before nightfall.

Gabriel sat up beside me and grabbed his shirt from off the floor beside the bed and slid it over his head. I ran my fingers through my ruffled hair while stifling a yawn. My stomach grumbled and I realized I hadn't eaten since leaving Daphne's place yesterday. We hadn't packed any food and had no money to buy some.

We put ourselves together quickly and came down the stairs rather sheepishly, as if we were two children who had just been caught doing something wrong.

Thalia was busy at the counter and she looked up with a sly grin on her face when she saw us. "Did you sleep well?" she asked coyly.

I felt my face heat up with embarrassment and I refused to look over at Gabriel. I could almost feel his gleeful smirk watching me as I fumbled over my words. "We slept very well, thank you," I said as firmly as I could but I knew Thalia would still think what she wanted to.

"We really appreciate your kindness."

"It was my pleasure. It's been far too long since I had guests here," she said. She held up a large potato sack and handed it to me. "I made a few things for you to bring with you."

Surprise filled me and I graciously accepted the bag, peeking inside at the contents. There was a loaf of fresh bread, some sausage wrapped in paper, along with a hunk of cheese. There was another canteen of water and a small bottle of rum.

"Thank you so much," I exclaimed. I placed the food inside my backpack, moved by Thalia's kindness.

"I wish you both all the best in your travels," she said, her eyes lighting up with a tiny sparkle.

I walked around the counter and wrapped my arms around the small woman. She smelled faintly of rum and fresh bread.

"You have no idea how much this means to us," I said.

Thalia gave me a gentle pat on the arm, looking up at me with a smile.

We began to make our way towards the door and I looked back over my shoulder to wave goodbye. Thalia waved back, looking rather forlorn to see us leave.

Once we were outside, Gabriel turned to me, unfolding the map he held in his hand. "If my estimates are correct, we should make it to the place where the Rose is supposedly located before sunset."

I felt my heart skip a beat, not wanting to get my hopes up too much. Today was the day of truth, the day I would find out whether the Rose was real or if it was only a legend. I didn't know what I expected to find or what exactly I would do once I had it.

My parents' lives and the fate of my kingdom rested on this Rose. Without it, the crown would fall into the hands of a power-hungry monster who cared only for himself.

I couldn't let that happen.

Gabriel reached over and wrapped his arms around me in a warm embrace, as if he could somehow make all my worries and fears go away. I wished he could.

I couldn't pretend any longer that everything was okay, that all my problems could be solved by a combination of temporary fixes. I needed to face the situation like the queen I had been raised to be, not the little girl I felt like inside.

"Gabriel, I haven't been totally honest with you," I admitted, pulling away from him and trying to steady the tremor in my voice.

"What do you mean?" he asked, his brow furrowing with confusion.

I began to walk down the dusty road, already feeling a trickle of sweat run down my neck from the hot sun blazing down on us.

"My name is not Ari," I said, watching his face closely to see his reaction. I didn't know what to say or how I could explain everything to him but I didn't want to lie anymore. No one could truly know me without knowing the crown that I served and the throne I would one day inherit.

"Well it is, sort of—" I stammered, trying to find the right words to say.

"What are you talking about?" asked Gabriel, his face growing pale.

My stomach dropped and I sucked in a deep breath before continuing. "My full name is Arianna Alexandra Quintis," I said.

"Quintis....?" repeated Gabriel, trying to find the missing piece to the puzzle in his mind.

"You mean...?" his voice trailed off and he looked at me as if he was seeing me for the first time.

"You're Princess Arianna?"

"Yes," I whispered, a lump forming in the back of my throat.

A mix of unreadable emotions flashed across his face. "Ari....?" he began but then stopped. "Or can I even call you that anymore? You've been lying to me all this time? I told you all about my past and yet you left out one of the biggest details about who you are!" he exclaimed angrily.

"Gabriel please," I choked out, tears welling up and stinging my eyes. "I'm still Ari! This doesn't change anything. I didn't want to tell you because I thought you would treat me differently. My crown doesn't change who I am."

"It changes everything," he said, his face falling.

I could see the pain in his eyes and I hated that I was the cause.

"I am still just a normal girl. I'm sorry I lied to you. I never intended to hurt you. I didn't even know all of this was going to happen and you were going to come with me." I threw my hands helplessly into the air, letting them fall to my sides.

"Why are you really here?" Gabriel asked me, accusingly.

"I didn't lie about my situation," I said. "My parents' lives and my kingdom are still at stake."

He looked deep into my eyes, as if he was trying to decide if I was telling the truth or not. "Why did you let me kiss you? Why did you lead me on and make me think that we could be something?"

"I never led you on or lied about how I feel," I cried.

Gabriel looked at me with a glimmer of tears in his eyes. "I thought we had something special."

"We do," I said adamantly, wishing I could make him understand. Wordlessly, I turned around and began to walk down the road, away from Gabriel. I could feel his eyes boring into me as the space began to grow between us.

I refused to turn around to look at him. I never asked for him to come with me. If he wanted to leave now, that was his choice to make.

The empty road stretched before me and I began to walk faster, already missing the feeling of having someone to walk beside, step after step, mile after mile. Now, I was all alone.

In some ways, I felt as if this was how it was meant to be all along. I had fallen twice for boys who had left me just as quickly as they had entered my life, taking pieces of my heart with them.

I half expected Gabriel to call out to me, to come running after me, to apologize and tell me that my crown didn't change anything between us. But he was right. It changed everything and we had been foolish and naive to believe this would work.

After a few minutes of walking, I finally stopped and allowed myself to turn around. I could faintly make out the outline of Gabriel's figure far down the road. Walking away. He was walking away from me. From *us*. From our future and what could have been. But none of that mattered anymore.

I straightened my back, standing taller and forced myself to keep walking, one foot in front of the other. Tears slid down my cheeks, quickly drying against my skin from the hot sun.

I didn't need anyone. I would finish this the same way I had started it.

Alone.

I neared the top of a large cliff, the faint sound of rushing water I had been following for several minutes quickly became a deafening, thunderous roar. I stopped at the edge, peering over to stare down into the swirling, raging abyss below. A large waterfall rushed under a rickety rope bridge that stretched across the canyon, flowing into the Raven River. My heart pounded in my chest, in time with the waves crashing against the jagged rocks and sticking out of the water.

"Just breathe," I whispered to myself, my words inaudible over the roaring sound of the waterfall.

It had only been a few hours since Gabriel had left me but the ache in my chest was still as strong as before. I was alone again, betrayed by the very person I thought I could trust, even after telling myself I would never let myself fall into that trap again.

It seemed I couldn't tell the difference between a wolf and sheep, despite many warnings not to trust anyone.

I glanced down at the weathered, dirt stained map I held in my shaky hands, tracing the path I had come and following the red line down to where I needed to go. The line crossed over the Raven River and then seemed to follow it to the mouth where it connected to the Aquarian Sea.

I felt excitement and fear simultaneously rise up within me at the thought of finally reaching my destination. I had crossed an ocean and traveled miles to get to this place, based only on an Oberian myth. There were no assurances that the Red Rose was actually real. There were no assurances that Draxon would actually keep his word and release my parents once he got the flower. I didn't even know how I was going to get back to Aurora or what I would do once I did.

I needed this to work. I needed the Rose to be real.

Gathering up my courage, I began to make my way down the cliff along a narrow and winding path to the start of the bridge which I would have to cross to get to the other side.

I dug my heels into the ground, trying to keep a foothold while running a hand along the rock face that lined the path in case I slipped. The palms of my hands were clammy and I could feel the sweat perspiring on my brow.

If I fell, there would be no one to catch me or pull me back up over the edge.

Making my way safely down the side, I reached the rope bridge, my relief quickly replaced with dread.

The bridge was dilapidated, the rope frayed and the boards rotten and broken. I gingerly placed one foot on the first rung of the bridge, feeling the board crack under my weight, as if it would give way at any moment.

My heart plummeted to my feet as I thought about one of the boards breaking. I pictured myself falling to my death on the rocks below. No one would ever know what had become of me.

I wondered how long Draxon would wait before he realized I was not coming back. Or maybe he had already assumed I would die on the journey.

There was no way I would let Draxon take the throne without a fight. I would not let him rob my father of the crown he had spent his whole life serving. My father had a heart for the good of his people but Draxon only cared about himself.

I scanned the map, looking to see if there was another way to get across the river. The bridge was the only way.

Preparing myself, I tucked the map inside my backpack, trying to still my racing heart.

I grabbed hold of the side of the bridge, my whole body trembling with fear. I tentatively put out my foot and set it down on the first board. I tested it to see if it would hold me before putting my whole weight on it and moving to the next board.

I could see gaping holes in the bridge up ahead, some spots missing two or three boards.

My hands were slick with sweat as I gripped the rope on either side of me as tightly as I could. I was innately aware of my surroundings and my fate if something went wrong. Blood pounded in my ears, in sync with the crashing of the waves against the rocks below. The wind whistled in my ears and swayed the bridge from side to side, giving me the illusion that someone was calling my name.

I blinked and tried to focus straight ahead. I took a large step to avoid a gaping hole where a board was missing. I sucked in a deep breath when I made it over, reassuring myself that everything was okay, that I was already halfway across.

"Ari!" I heard the persistent voice again.

I slowly turned around to look behind me. My heart leapt to my throat and tears welled up in the backs of my eyes.

"What are you doing here, Gabriel?"

"Ari, stop! Don't move! I'm coming." Gabriel put one foot on the first board and then another, beginning to make his way towards me.

"I'm sorry I lied to you, Gabriel. I know I should have told you who I was but—"

A loud cracking noise echoed across the ravine and I froze, too scared to move. There was another crack, louder this time and I felt the board shift beneath me.

"Gabriel," I said quietly, trying to remain calm.

"Don't move," he said, our eyes meeting.

A flash of fear crossed his face as he continued to make his way across the bridge, trying not to shake the bridge and make it even more unstable.

Suddenly, the board cracked and I felt it give out beneath me. I screamed and clutched onto the rope railing. My feet dangled in the open air above the water and I could feel the foamy spray on my face.

"Help!" I cried in utter terror.

I felt the bridge shaking as Gabriel ran towards me, jumping over the gaping holes in the bridge.

"Give me your hand," exclaimed Gabriel, finally reaching me and holding out his hand. I grabbed onto it like a lifeline, trying to pull myself back up onto the boards.

There was another menacing crack from the added weight on the bridge and I felt Gabriel let go of my hand as the board gave out beneath him.

There was only empty air and the sound of our screams echoing across the ravine as we fell.

Chapter 17

I hit the water. Hard. Icy pinpricks from the frigid river jabbed my body like knives. My chest constricted and I fought for air. My clothing and leather boots weighed me down and I fought desperately to the surface. My hair was matted across my face and I coughed and spluttered, trying to get the water out of my lungs.

I thrashed in the swirling river, frantically searching for Gabriel. Panic rose within me and an image of Gabriel lying lifeless in the water only a few nights before flashed through my mind. I thought I had lost him once. I couldn't let that happen again.

The raging river showed me no mercy as I was swept downstream. I tried to avoid the jagged rocks sticking up. The waves splashed up and over my head, the sound of the water roaring in my ears as I tried to fight the current and find a way to shore.

I caught sight of a rock that jutted out of the water and I tried to grab onto it. My hands slipped as water washed over it repeatedly. I was pulled further downstream, struggling to stay afloat. I felt the cold in my bones and a dull, hollow ache spreading through my limbs as the energy slowly seeped out of me.

"Gabriel," I choked out in a garbled voice. I knew there was no use in calling him because he would never be able to hear me over the sound of the falls.

I paddled down the river, holding my head as far above the water as possible.

Out of the corner of my eye, I saw a large branch hanging out over the water from a nearby tree. Hope surged through me, giving me a sudden burst of adrenaline. I paddled hard and attempted to swim towards it. A large wave pushed me in sideways, close enough to allow me to grab hold of the branch.

I tried to pull myself up onto the shore, using the branch for leverage. A sharp pain shot through my arm as I held on with all my strength, the water grabbing at my legs and trying to suck me back into the current.

I dug my fingers into the damp earth on the embankment, frustration building up inside of me as I pulled away a chunk of dirt in my hands. I pressed my hand further down into the dirt, still holding onto the branch with the other.

Sucking in a deep breath, trying to settle the churning feeling in the pit of my stomach, I let go of the branch and pulled myself up onto the bank. I flopped onto my side, heart racing. I breathed in the smell of the damp earth, felt the cool grass against my skin and gazed up at the blue sky.

Somehow I was alive.

But where was Gabriel? My relief was short-lived as raw fear filled me yet again. I quickly got to my feet, scanning the tumultuous waters for any sign of him.

"Gabriel!" I screamed. A wave of dizziness swept over me and black spots danced at the edge of my vision. I closed my eyes for a couple of seconds until the spinning stopped.

"Gabriel!" I called again. I had almost lost him so many times and tried to imagine what it would be like if he was really gone. But he always came back.

I couldn't lose him now.

I hobbled downstream where the current ran faster as it neared the falls. Anything or anyone sucked into its grasp would plummet to their death on the jagged rocks below.

Out of the corner of my eye, I thought I caught a glimpse of a head, bobbing in the water. Squinting against the bright sunlight, I got as close as I could to the edge of the bank, frantically searching the water.

"Gabriel!" I yelled, desperately hoping that if he was nearby, he would hear my call.

My heart jumped to my throat as I spotted him, thrashing and flailing in the water as he was swept downstream. I froze, feeling my body grow cold with fear as my mind spun with what to do.

I searched the tree-lined shore for a sturdy branch that would be able to support Gabriel's weight. There was a big branch from a maple tree that I dragged towards the river's edge, praying this would work.

"Gabriel!" I held the branch out as far over the river as I could reach, hoping he would see it in time before he was swept farther away.

He turned his head, looking around him as water splashed up in his face, trying to locate me.

"Over here!" I exclaimed, waving the branch in an effort to catch his eye.

Catching sight of me, he attempted to paddle closer to shore, working against the current as it continued to pull him closer to the falls. The branch was just beyond his reach and he tried to push himself closer to shore by kicking off of a rock to gain some momentum.

My breath caught in the back of my throat as his fingers grazed the edge of the branch, taking a few stray leaves away in his fist. He quickly reached for it again, this time grabbing hold of a thicker part of the branch and clinging for his life.

I began to walk backwards, pulling on the branch as hard as I could as I tried to get Gabriel back on dry land. Once he was touching the bank, I dropped the branch and knelt down beside the river. I grabbed his arms and placed them around my neck, straining under his weight as I lifted him and laid him down in the grass.

I collapsed at his side and cupped his cheek in my hand. I could feel his breath against my hand and see his chest rising as he sucked in deep gulps of fresh air. He coughed and sputtered as he tried to clear the water from his lungs.

"Thank you, thank you, thank you," I murmured as I stared at the man before me.

"Ari," whispered Gabriel, reaching out his hand to brush a wet lock of hair from my eyes. "Thank *you*. You saved my life today."

I leaned down without thinking and pressed my lips gently against his. My heart fluttered in my chest and I felt heat rise inside of me as I wrapped my arms around his neck.

I reluctantly pulled away, looking down at Gabriel to see his reaction. The familiar sparkle I loved had returned to his hazel eyes and some colour had crept its way back into his cheeks. He slowly sat up and placed his hands gently around my waist, pulling me to him again.

I wrapped my arms around him and held on. Everytime I tried to let Gabriel go, I felt like I was giving away a piece of myself.

I didn't want to let him go again.

"We should probably continue on if we are going to find this Rose," said Gabriel, breaking the embrace.

"You're right," I said, wrapping my arms around myself as my teeth began to chatter.

"Do you still have the map?" he asked.

I pulled my sopping wet backpack off my shoulders and set it on the ground with a thud. "I don't know if it will be of much use to us now or if it's even still intact," I said.

I opened up my bag and removed the blanket we had brought with us from Daphne's place. I tossed aside the paper bag Thalia had given us with some fresh bread and cheese, bits of wet paper coming away in my hands.

I pulled out the little velvet bag that held the compass, thankful it had something to protect it from the water. I set it gently to the side, noticing Gabriel's inquisitive gaze as his eyes flickered from it to me.

Finally, I produced the dripping wet cloth that was our map, my heart sinking as I saw the faded colours as the ink all ran together.

"It's okay, Ari," said Gabriel, "I was looking at the map earlier and I'm pretty sure we just have to follow the Raven River downstream and there should be a cave where the Rose is."

I looked at him skeptically. "Are you sure?" I asked, trying to create a visual image of the map in my head.

"Trust me," he said, slinging an arm over my shoulder. "We're going to find this Rose."

I felt my lips twitch as a small smile slid across my face. "I hope so." I leaned down to grab the little bag with the compass, leaving my backpack and the rest of its contents behind since they were dripping wet and served little purpose for us now.

"What's that?" asked Gabriel.

I undid the drawstring and pulled out the compass, the gold glinting in the sunlight. I heard Gabriel suck in a deep breath beside me.

"Draxon gave this to me. It's supposed to help us find the Rose." I tapped the glass that protected the rose in the center. The extended petal moved ever so slightly, pointing straight ahead.

"Are you sure it works?"

"I don't know," I replied, shrugging my shoulders. "We'll find out though."

I led the way downstream with Gabriel following in my footsteps. Today was the day I would know whether everything Draxon had told me was a lie or if the Rose was actually real. My future and the lives of my parents and my people depended on it.

The sunlight was beginning to wane, even though I guessed it was still early in the afternoon. Dark storm clouds were gathering overhead and the air felt sticky. My damp clothes clung to my skin and I felt beads of sweat run down the back of my neck.

"If I remember the map correctly, the cave should be just around this—"

I stopped abruptly in my tracks, pulse pounding. "There it is," I whispered, my gaze landing on a large opening in the rock at the mouth of the river.

"Are you ready to do this?" asked Gabriel, watching my face intently.

I felt an unexpected lurch in my stomach. Now that the moment of truth had arrived, I wasn't sure I was ready to face it. But I had to. For my parents. And my people. And myself. This was what would secure my role as princess of Oberia and my future as their queen.

"Yes. I'm going in. *Alone*," I emphasized.

"Ari, please. It might not be safe. I'll come with you," insisted Gabriel, putting a gentle hand on my shoulder.

I brushed it away. "No," I said firmly. "Please Gabriel, I need to do this by myself."

He stepped back and let me pass him as I approached the cave. Sucking in a deep breath, I stepped into the blackness. The sound of water dripping echoed against stone and I felt the immediate coolness envelop me as the sun was blocked out by rock. A bit of light still filtered in from the entrance. I surveyed the cavernous space as my eyes adjusted, immediately noticing it was empty.

"There's nothing here," I called out, feeling my voice beginning to break as I tried to maintain my composure. There was nothing. This realization brought on an overpowering sense of defeat.

"Look around. There could be a hidden room or another part of the cave," he called in to me.

Frustrated and not sure where to even begin looking, I began to run my hand along the wall of the cave, searching for any special grooves in the wall or some sort of marking that would indicate this was where the Rose was located.

The stone felt cool to the touch and my footsteps echoed in the air as I circled the cave.

I had not come all this way to return home in defeat.

"Any luck?" called Gabriel from outside.

"None," I said, trying to hold back the tears welling up inside of me.

I heard footsteps behind me and I whirled around to see Gabriel walking towards me. "Let me help you," he pleaded. "You don't have to do this all alone."

"I know," I said, giving in.

"Can I see the compass for a minute?" asked Gabriel.

I handed him the velvet bag, questions filling my mind. "I doubt that will help," I said.

"You never know."

He pulled the compass out of the bag and I watched as the petal slowly began to spin, faster and faster until it finally slowed down and pointed at the wall across from us.

I looked at Gabriel, not sure what to make of it. "That was weird. The compass rose has hardly moved since Draxon gave it to me."

"I think it means something," he said, walking over to the adjacent cave wall, letting his hand trail along it.

I scanned the rock, not sure what he expected to find.

"Ari," he breathed, his hand hovering over an indent in the cave wall.

"What is it?" I asked, peering over his shoulder to see what he had found.

My heart skipped a beat as I saw the outline of a compass carved into the wall with a rose in the center. Gabriel gently placed the compass into the wall and took a step back to see what would happen. The cave was eerily quiet and all I could hear was the faint drip of water and my own racing heart.

Suddenly, there was a loud scraping sound as the stone wall in front of us began to slowly move to the side to reveal a hidden room behind it.

"Gabriel!" I exclaimed, jumping up and down excitedly. "This is it! The Red Rose is in here, I know it!"

His eyes were wide and his mouth fell open as he looked from me to the room and back again. "I didn't think it would actually work," he said with disbelief."

I laughed and grabbed his arm, pulling him into the room with me. As I rounded the corner, I saw a faint red glow. Heart hammering in my chest, I let go of Gabriel's arm and ventured deeper into the room that continued far back into the rock.

I held my breath as the light grew brighter, and the room became more illuminated. I stopped in my tracks and I felt Gabriel rest a hand on my shoulder and suck in a deep breath.

"The Red Rose….we found it…."

"*You* found it," Gabriel murmured.

The Rose stood under a glass dome, floating in the space within. It sat on a large, stone table, covered in ancient writing.

Suddenly, I felt an all too familiar stabbing, searing pain in my arm and I clutched it with a cry of pain.

"Ari, are you okay?" asked Gabriel, looking down at my arm with confusion.

I gingerly rolled up my sleeve to reveal the mark of the Rose that was glowing bright red.

Gabriel leapt back, his eyes wide. "What is happening?"

"I don't know!" I exclaimed. "This is what happened to me before when we were on the ship."

"Draxon said this was how he knew you were the one that had to get the Red Rose," he muttered to himself, his brow furrowing with thought.

I gritted my teeth together, trying to forget about the feeling of fire burning in my veins. I watched as Gabriel began to pace, then hesitantly took a few steps towards the Rose.

"What are you doing, Gabriel?"

He didn't reply but continued to inch his way closer to the stone table. He slowly stretched out his arm towards it but was suddenly thrown backwards onto the ground a few feet away.

Letting my arm fall to my side, I ran to Gabriel and knelt on the cave floor beside him.

"Are you okay? What happened?" I asked, trying to process what was going on.

Gabriel rubbed the back of his head, gingerly getting back on his feet. "There must be some kind of force field around the Rose. It won't let me get near it."

"This must be why I had to come," I said, the realization hitting me for the first time. "How is this possible?"

"I guess that's why they call it *magic*," said Gabriel, shock evident on his face.

It was a lot to take in. Somehow, I was special, the only person who could get the Rose. I felt a shiver run down my spine as my nerves twisted into tiny knots I didn't know if I would ever get undone.

I took a step forward, eyes fixed on the Rose. The red pulsating light seemed simultaneously haunting and beautiful. I let my hands fall loosely at my sides and I walked almost on tiptoe, as if at any moment I would be thrown back like Gabriel.

I held my breath as I stood in front of it, hand hovering over the glass dome that protected the Rose from falling into the wrong hands.

Hands like Draxon's that I planned to place the Rose in. Hands that had the power to kill my parents if I didn't do this.

I lifted the glass dome, setting it gently on the stone table and reached for the Rose. Blood thrummed in my ears, drowning out the sound of my own ragged breathing and the dripping of water echoing off the cave walls. The Rose felt almost weightless in my hands, the petals soft and cool to the touch.

But a weight pressed down on my heart, locking away my conscience that tried to make me consider the consequences. If Draxon didn't keep his word, my parents would be killed and my people would be doomed to a life under his iron fist.

I couldn't stand by and watch Draxon wear my father's crown. But I couldn't defy him and risk my parents' lives either. I had the Rose and that was all that mattered. Once I made it home, I would figure out what to do.

Suddenly, I felt a sharp prick in my back just below my neck and I could feel cold metal digging into my skin.

"Don't move," came a firm, menacing voice.

My heart dropped into my stomach and my body immediately turned to ice.

"Gabriel?"

Chapter 18

I slowly turned around, my eyes meeting Gabriel's. It was like staring into a dark, hollow abyss, unlike the familiar twinkle I had grown to love.

He held a dagger in his hand and I could feel the cold metal pressed against my skin through my thin cotton shirt. I could see the veins in his hand as he gripped it, no sign of a tremor.

My head spun as I stared back at Gabriel, trying to understand what was going on. "What are you doing?" I choked out, my voice shaking.

I watched as he clenched and then unclenched his jaw and his face flushed a deep red. "Give me the Rose," he said through gritted teeth.

"What?" I gasped, shaking my head and blinking, as if I was hallucinating. "Gabriel, what are you doing? I don't understand."

He took a small step forward and I could feel the dagger prick the surface of my skin ever so slightly. I winced and my heart felt like it was going to jump out of my chest.

"Give me the Rose," Gabriel repeated, his eyes narrowing as he looked at me.

A wave of nausea washed over me and my stomach roiled. I swallowed, trying to get rid of the bile that rose in the back of my throat. This couldn't be happening. I had trusted Gabriel and opened my heart to him, believing he wouldn't break it like Darian had.

How could I have been wrong again?

"Gabriel, please tell me what is going on?" My gaze flickered from the dagger pressed against my chest to his eyes, searching them for any sign of the boy I knew was in there.

I watched as he shifted from foot to foot. His grip on the dagger wavered so slightly, I wondered if I had imagined it.

"If you just give me the Rose, it will be a whole lot easier for both of us," he said, swallowing nervously.

My stomach sank and I felt a tear slide down my cheek and I tasted salt on my lips. "Gabriel, you know this is the only way I can save my family! I told you everything about who I am and what I'm trying to do. My family and my country are doomed without this!" My voice rose as I grew more hysterical. The tears came faster, dripping down my neck and onto my shirt, still wet from the river.

I saw the faintest glimmer of tears in Gabriel's eyes but he blinked them away before they could fall.

"I don't want to do this, Ari," he whispered.

"Do what?" I cried. "I don't understand! I thought you—" I stopped abruptly, refusing to let my next words cross my lips.

"You thought I what…?" asked Gabriel, a flicker of fear passing over his face.

I looked down at the Rose in my hand, focusing on the pulsating red glow that continued to emanate from its petals.

"I thought you loved me," I said, my voice breaking as sobs wracked my whole body.

I thought I knew what heartbreak was when Darian had thrown Gabriel overboard. I thought he was the bad guy, the one I had foolishly given my heart too. I had vowed that I would never open my heart to another person again.

But I had chosen to break the promise I had made to myself. I had chosen to let Gabriel in. The kiss we had shared, the secrets I had told, the hope I had let myself hold onto that he might love me had all been a lie.

I felt his hand on my chin, his touch gentle as he lifted my chin, forcing me to look into his eyes. I tried to pull away but he tightened his grip on my jaw. The seconds dragged by as time stood still.

"I didn't want to fall in love with you," he murmured, his breath warm and sweet against my face.

My heart skipped a beat and I tried to steady my breathing. Words rushed to my lips as I opened my mouth to speak but I froze and pushed them away.

"It wasn't an accident that I tried to rob you that day at the wharf. I knew exactly who you were and what you were doing there."

Gabriel continued to hold my gaze as he spoke and I was very aware of the dagger still pressed into my skin, waiting to be driven into my chest if I tried to run away.

"I wandered into a tavern about a month ago, planning to drink the night away. There was a man sitting on a stool at the counter and he was watching me. He bought me a drink and started asking me about my life."

As I listened to Gabriel talk, I felt as if I was walking through a dark, misty forest, unable to see anything except my hand in front of my face. I had no idea what he was talking about or where he was going with this. *How did he know who I was and that I was going to be at the wharf?*

"The man told me he had a brother who was greedy and hungry for power and wealth. His brother had cheated him out of his family inheritance by lying to their parents and had him cut off." Gabriel looked at me with an unreadable expression on his face, as if he was watching for my reaction.

"He told me there was a magical flower that would help him to go back in the past and change what happened. He could fix the damage his brother had caused and regain the inheritance that was rightfully his. He promised me money and a chance at a good life if I would get this flower for him…." His voice trailed off and he looked down at his feet.

My heart jumped inside of me as I finally realized what Gabriel was talking about.

"You're working for Draxon. He wanted you to follow me and befriend me so I would lead you to the Rose and you would bring it back to him. He never intended to let me or my parents live. You came here to kill me," I murmured to myself, everything finally coming together, like pieces from a puzzle.

I looked up at Gabriel to see a few stray tears run down his cheeks. "Ari, I thought you were the bad guy. Draxon led me to believe you and your family had robbed him of his inheritance and didn't care about anyone but yourselves. I thought I was doing the right thing. I had no idea you were the princess or I would have known Draxon was lying. You have to believe me."

"Gabriel," I said, cold anger hardening my heart, "you've lied to me so many times, I don't know what to believe. Has everything been a lie from the beginning? Everything you told me about your past, your feelings for me, our kiss?"

I wanted to believe Gabriel was the victim here, that he had been lied to and never intended to harm me but that was only my emotions affecting my judgement.

"At first it was an act but once I got to know you, I wanted to tell you the truth. I never lied to you about how I felt. I didn't expect to fall in love with you…. but I did." He looked at me with those wide hazel eyes of his, wanting me to believe him, to forgive him for everything he had done.

But he had betrayed me and I wouldn't let myself get hurt again.

"Why didn't you tell me the truth? Why did you decide to go through with it?" I looked from his face down to the dagger against my chest.

The silence stretched between us and my heart raced, waiting for him to reply.

"I guess there was still a part of me that wanted another chance at life. A chance to have a mother and father who loved me."

A piece of my heart broke for him and I saw him for who he really was— a little boy who only wanted to belong.

But he had lied to me and put my life and the lives of my parents and my people at risk. He was my enemy. He had chosen his side and I would not let him stand in my way.

In one swift motion I wrenched the dagger out of his hand and shoved him against the cave wall. I could feel his chest heaving beneath my arm and I saw a flicker of fear in his eyes.

I held my hand steady, feeling the cold metal in my clammy hand, the Rose still clenched tightly in the other as I held the blade against Gabriel's chest. I could feel his hot breath on my face as I let my eyes bore into him. My heart hammered inside of me and I could faintly make out the sound of the river outside the cave.

It was as if time had come to a halt and there was only me and Gabriel and the dagger between us. One thrust and he would be done for.

Images of Gabriel lying next to me, the feeling of his lips pressed against mine flashed through my mind. Memories of our water fight on the ship when he was supposed to be mopping or him running towards me on the bridge before we fell filled my thoughts.

I felt a deep, hollow ache in my chest as I looked into Gabriel's eyes, those eyes that had once looked at me with what I thought was love.

Everything that had happened between us was a lie. I choked back the sob that rose in my throat and steeled myself for what I had to do.

I pressed the blade a bit harder into his skin, watching as Gabriel winced. My hand began to tremble despite my best efforts to conceal it. Red slowly seeped through his thin cotton shirt, leaving a small, dark stain.

I let the dagger fall to the ground with a clatter against the wet stone. Gabriel stood motionless, staring at me and then down at the blade between us.

"Just kill me," he whispered, his face void of emotion.

Tears blurred my vision but I brushed them away before they could fall.

"No," I said firmly. "You deserve to die but I don't want your blood on my hands. I would rather you live the rest of your life remembering this moment with regret."

I gave him one last long look before picking up the dagger and turning back towards the cave entrance.

"If I ever see you again, I won't hesitate to kill you." My icy words hung in the air, echoing off the cave walls.

I lowered the dagger, turning my back on Gabriel for the last time. I could hear my footsteps echoing off the stone as I walked away from the boy I thought I had loved.

I slowly breathed in and out, holding myself together by a thread until I stepped into the fresh air and waning sunlight. I let the tears fall freely as I began to walk back the way I had come.

I had gotten what I came for but somehow, it still felt like I was leaving everything behind.

Chapter 19

I will kill him. I will kill him. I kept repeating this promise over and over in my head, in rhythm with my footsteps and my pounding heart.

"I *will* kill Draxon."

The dark, hollow look I had seen in Gabriel's eyes in the cave was the same empty look I had seen in Draxon's eyes. I knew the boy I had loved was still inside Gabriel somewhere but there was only a monster inside of Draxon, waiting to devour anyone who stood in his way.

When the time came, I would look him in the eye, plunge the dagger into his chest and watch him bleed out on the cold stone floor of the palace. And I would feel no remorse.

I let my anger and my desire for revenge worm its way into my heart and eat away at my conscience, at the part of myself that had always been told to repay evil with good.

I didn't care what the right thing was. Draxon deserved to die.

"I will kill him." I let my words ring out over the river and through the trees as I walked.

Draxon thought I was disposable, someone who could be used to get what he wanted and then killed off once I had served my purpose.

But I wasn't that girl. Maybe I had been a few weeks ago when I left the palace but not anymore.

I would stand up to Draxon, regardless of the consequences. He couldn't break my heart if there wasn't anything left to break.

I walked through the night, not wanting to stop because that was when my thoughts would take over. I needed to get back to the palace as soon as possible and I had no idea what I was going to do when I got there. I didn't even know if there would be a ship going back to Aurora or if I would need to stay and wait a few days for the next one to come. But I didn't have time to waste.

The sun was just beginning to peek over the tops of the trees and the darkness was covered up with streaks of red, orange, and yellow, like brush strokes on a painter's canvas. Up ahead, I caught a glimpse of a familiar, rickety building that looked as if it was leaning precariously to one side.

I stopped in my tracks as memories of coming here with Gabriel flooded my mind. I tried to block out the feeling of being in his arms as he carried me up the stairs or the feeling of his lips against mine. All those long hours of conversation when he had shared about his past. I didn't know what was the truth and what was lies.

I slowly made my way towards the tavern, hoping that Thalia wouldn't ask about Gabriel. If she did, I knew I would break down and I didn't know if I would be able to put myself together again.

The sound of voices rang out in the quiet forest that surrounded the building. I could faintly make out Thalia's hoarse, raspy voice along with another, younger, deeper sounding voice. I paused on the porch outside, wondering if I should just continue on. But exhaustion weighed my body down and a dull, hollow ache filled my legs. There was nowhere else to stop along the way unless I wanted to sleep outside with the wild animals.

I grabbed the door handle and pushed, caught off guard by the feeling of someone pulling against the door on the other side to open it. I fell forward into the tavern as the door swung open and I felt someone grab me by the arm to stop me from falling.

"Thank you," I mumbled, flustered by my less than graceful entrance, knowing I probably looked dirty and disheveled.

"Ari?" came a voice that set my heart and mind to racing.

I looked up slowly, into the sea-green eyes of the boy I thought I would never see again.

"Darian," I whispered, swallowing around the lump in my throat.

Out of the corner of my eye, I saw Thalia approach, hands on her hips, wearing a flour-covered apron.

"Well, I'll be darned," she said, looking at me with a small twinkle in her eyes. "I never thought I would see you again. Do you two know each other?" she asked, looking between Darian and I with confusion.

"What happened to the other boy you were with?" Thalia asked, peering out the window, as if expecting him to be waiting somewhere outside.

My throat felt as if it had been stuffed with cotton balls and I didn't know what to say. After letting the silence stretch awkwardly between us, I finally got up the nerve to address Darian.

"What are you doing here?" My tone sounded more accusatory than I meant it to but the last thing I needed was my emotions getting in the way of my logic yet again.

"I was looking for you," he answered, his eyes gazing deep into mine.

I felt a rush of anger well up inside of me. "I told you before that I don't need you to protect me, Darian. Why don't you understand that?"

Pain flickered across his face. "I can't change my feelings for you. I know you must hate me for everything that has happened, but I never wanted to hurt you." His gaze moved from my face to the Rose dangling from my left hand and the dagger I carried in the other.

"You found it," he said, and I could hear the shock in his voice.

I nodded. "I got what I needed and now I'm heading back home."

Darian shifted his weight between his feet and looked as if he was trying to decide what to say next.

"Come child and get something to eat. You must be starved," said Thalia, interrupting our exchange.

Relief filled me as she wrapped her arms around me and led me over the counter and helped me sit down on a stool.

Darian stayed by the door, glancing awkwardly over at us. I kept my eyes on the battered counter, studying the water rings from where people had placed their glasses or slammed them down a little too hard.

I never wanted or expected to see Darian again. Only a few days had passed since we were on the ship together, but in some ways, it felt like it had been months. So much had happened and I wasn't ready to let anyone see the broken parts of me.

Thalia emerged with some bread, cheese, and sausage she had thrown together along with a mug of herbal tea. I graciously accepted both, sucking in a deep breath as the steam filled my nose.

"I'll be in the back if you need anything," she said, giving my hand a loving pat before leaving me alone with Darian.

I felt my body tense as I heard footsteps behind me and the sound of a stool scraping against the wood floor as Darian sat down beside me.

"Are you going to tell me what happened?"

"No," I answered firmly.

I could feel Darian's eyes on me as I bit into the bread, still warm from the oven.

"I once knew a girl who wanted to let me in, who told me things she had never told anyone before."

My heart skipped a beat and I gripped my mug tightly as my anger turned to sadness.

"I once knew a boy who I trusted with my heart but then he shattered it into a million tiny pieces."

I heard Darian shift uncomfortably beside me and then I felt his hand on my shoulder. I jerked away as if I had been burned, sloshing some of my tea on the counter.

"Get your hands off of me," I growled.

"Ari, please," begged Darian and I could see a glimmer of tears in his eyes as he spoke. "You don't understand….back on the ship, when Gabriel fell overboard—"

"You mean the night you threw him overboard!" I interrupted angrily, my voice rising to a shout.

"No Ari," said Darian, looking me in the eye. "The night of the storm, I caught him lurking outside of your room and I asked him what he was doing. He acted all flustered and caught off guard and wouldn't tell me. I told him that if he didn't tell me then I would report him to Captain Carter. I didn't trust him and I had an uneasy feeling I just couldn't shake. I walked away because I didn't want to start a fight but he followed me and shoved me up against the railing. He threatened to kill me if I told anyone about seeing him outside of your room. Then I guess you saw the rest," Darian finished, letting his voice trail off.

Images of Darian holding Gabriel up against the railing and then throwing him over the side flashed through my mind repeatedly. I didn't know what to believe anymore. Clearly Gabriel wasn't the good guy I thought he was. Darian had been right not to trust him. But I still wasn't sure if I could trust Darian either. Both boys had betrayed me and I didn't want anything to do with either.

"Where is Gabriel now?" asked Darian softly, probing for the story I kept locked inside of me.

I took another sip of my tea, to try to soothe the butterflies that danced inside of me. "I don't know," I answered honestly. I had left him back in the cave and I knew he wouldn't follow me. He was on his own again.

Darian raised his brows in question, clearly skeptical of my reply but he didn't press the matter further. My eyes followed his hand as he toyed with the violin pendant that hung around his wrist. The only piece he had of his mother.

My eyes began to water as I thought of my own mother, picturing every line in her face, the way her eyes creased when she smiled, the stray wisp of grey hair that always fell in her eyes when she laughed. I remembered her rose perfume and how a little bit of the scent would cling to my clothes after I gave her a hug.

All I wanted was to run into my mother's arms and never let go.

Not wanting to break down in front of Darian, I pushed back the stool and got to my feet. "I have to go," I said.

"No Ari, you need to stay here and rest. You're exhausted. We can leave later today once you've had a few hours of sleep."

I looked at Darian with disbelief, wondering when he would get it through his head that there was no *we*.

"I am going alone. I've made it this far without your help so I'm sure I can make it the rest of the way," I snapped.

"I guess we've reached an impasse then," said Darian, his mouth drawn into a thin, taut line.

"What do you mean?" I asked.

"You don't want me to come with you but I refuse to leave until I make sure you and your family are safe."

I slammed my fist down on the counter in frustration. "I am not your responsibility and neither is my family. Besides, Draxon will kill you if you come with me."

His gaze did not waver and I knew my words had done nothing to change his mind.

"Come child," said Thalia, suddenly emerging from the back room and gesturing for me to follow her.

A wave of tiredness swept over me and I knew there was no point in continuing on until I had gotten some rest. I turned my back on Darian and let her lead me upstairs to the small bedroom where Gabriel and I had slept only two nights ago.

I flopped down on the bed and buried my head in the pillow.

"There, there child," soothed Thalia, gently rubbing my back as sobs tore through my body. "Tell me what's wrong."

I couldn't. How could I possibly tell her everything that had gone horribly wrong in my life in the past month?

"It's about that dark haired fellow who stayed here the other night, isn't it?" prodded Thalia.

"There was never anything between us," I said with a hiccup. I propped myself up on one elbow and swiped at the tears that continued to fall down my cheeks and onto the pillow.

"Could have fooled me," quipped Thalia with a smirk. "I know love when I see it." Her voice trailed off and a faraway look entered her eyes. "And I also know heartbreak."

"He lied to me," I said. "He wouldn't have lied to me if he really loved me."

"Sometimes, people do foolish things when they are in love," replied Thalia, tucking a blonde wisp of hair behind my ear and giving my cheek a tender pat. "A man will do anything to protect the woman he loves."

"I wouldn't exactly call putting a dagger to my chest protecting me," I muttered under my breath.

"What was that?" asked Thalia, tilting her head with confusion.

I swiped the air with my hand. "Nothing," I said.

Thalia didn't even know Gabriel. And I didn't know him either. I thought he genuinely cared about me and wanted to help me save my family. But really, the only reason he stayed with me the whole time was because Draxon had promised him money and a future, a future that didn't include me.

"Don't become bitter over this," said Thalia softly. "I don't know what happened between you two but when you came into my tavern, I knew there was something special between you. I haven't seen a man look at a woman the way he looked at you for a long time. It's easy to lie with your words, but a person's eyes always tell the truth."

I twirled a strand of hair around my finger, wrapping it tighter and tighter and then letting it come unraveled.

"I'll let you get some sleep now," said Thalia, getting to her feet with a creak and a snap of brittle bone.

"Thank you," I murmured, already feeling my eyes drifting shut.

"What should I do about the man downstairs?" asked Thalia. "Should I ask him to leave?"

"No, let him stay if he wants to," I said.

"Okay," replied Thalia, a small smile creeping into her voice. "I don't think that young gentleman is going anywhere without you."

I felt a whisper of a smile creep onto my own face at the thought of Darian pacing the tavern below us, waiting for me to come back down and talk to him.

If he was willing to come all this way and wait for me, not even knowing if I would speak to him, then a few more hours of waiting wouldn't kill him.

Thalia was right. Darian would still be there, waiting for me whenever I was ready. Ready for what, I wasn't sure. To talk, to forgive, to offer him a second chance…. But I knew he would never walk away like Gabriel had.

Even when I had given him every reason to stay, Gabriel still chose to leave. And that was the worst kind of betrayal, having offered someone everything you had, and it still wasn't enough.

Chapter 20

I awoke to a crash of thunder and the sound of rain pounding on the roof above me. My eyes flew open and flickered back and forth, trying to make sense of where I was. After a long moment, the memories of being in the cave with Gabriel, a dagger pressed against my chest, came back with a dull ache. I was back at Thalia's Tavern and Darian was downstairs waiting for me.

I sat up groggily in bed, a small whimper escaping my lips. Every bone and muscle in my body burned with pain. I had walked through the whole night, after nearly dying twice, and now I was paying for it.

I ran my fingers through my hair and rubbed the sleep from my eyes, trying to make myself somewhat presentable. I had no idea how long I had been asleep for. Dark clouds blocked out the sun and a bolt of lightning streaked across the sky.

My stomach sank as I thought about how I was supposed to travel through that to get back to the harbour. No ships would be leaving in that kind of weather.

I tossed the blankets to the side and climbed out of bed, knowing it was time to face Darian. I didn't want to tell him the truth but I knew he wouldn't leave until I did.

I made my way downstairs, the boards creaking under my feet. As I rounded the corner, my heart skipped a beat. I could see the back of Darian's head as he sat on a stool at the counter, bottle of rum in hand as he talked with Thalia. Their voices were hushed and I couldn't make out what they were saying.

I saw Thalia nod her head in my direction and Darian swiveled on the stool to face me.

"Ari," he said, a small smile lighting up his face. "How did you sleep?"

"Really well," I said. "What time is it?"

"It's almost two o'clock," answered Thalia, motioning to a clock that hung on the wall behind me, it's glass face cracked.

"Why didn't someone wake me? I've been asleep for hours!" I exclaimed in frustration. I had made it back to the tavern just after dawn and had already wasted most of the day.

"I need to go," I said, starting to make my way towards the door.

Darian grabbed my arm and pulled me towards the counter. "In that?" he asked, incredulously. "Ari, you're exhausted and trying to travel in the middle of a thunderstorm is not going to get you anywhere."

"I don't even know if my parents are dead or alive so forgive me if I am anxious to get going," I spat, eyes flashing angrily.

"You won't be much help to them if you get yourself killed in the process," Darian said, his eyes flickering to the Rose and the dagger in my hands.

"I'll get you something to eat," said Thalia. "There's no use traveling on an empty stomach." She waddled away into the back room, leaving me alone with Darian, his hand still holding onto my arm.

I jerked it away, glaring at him before grudgingly sitting down on the stool next to him.

"Ari, please forgive me?" begged Darian, hands clasped together in front of him on the counter. "I can't even begin to imagine everything you've been through since you left home. I know you don't trust me and I understand why, but I want you to know that I care about you and I don't want you to do this alone. Not because I don't think you can do it but because I wouldn't be able to live with myself if I let you go."

My eyes grew glassy as he spoke and suddenly, my arms were wrapped tightly around him. I laid my head against his shoulder, breathing in the scent of sweat and rum. My mind flashed back to the night we had spent together in the crows nest, when I had first opened up to him and let him see a tiny piece of my childhood. And then only a few nights before we arrived in Destin, when Darian had kissed me and told me he didn't want to let me go.

Now, here I was, in the arms of the man who was still there, holding on, the one constant in my life when everything else was falling apart.

"Thank you," I murmured into his ear.

"For what?" he asked, gently rubbing my back.

"For coming to look for me, for not leaving me even when I asked you to…." I let my voice trail off as tears choked out my words.

"I could never leave you, Ari," Darian whispered, brushing away a loose wisp of hair and planting a soft kiss on my forehead.

"I need to tell you something," I confessed, slowly sitting up and pulling away from his embrace.

Darian looked back at me, eyes wide with concern.

"I haven't been totally honest with you about who I am." I paused as I watched Darian's face change from worried to confused, his eyes narrowing slightly.

"My full name is Arianna Alexandra Quintis," I said, letting out a deep breath.

Darian's jaw dropped and he ran a hand through his hair. "You mean, you're the princess?" he exclaimed incredulously.

I nodded, trying to gauge Darian's emotions.

"Draxon, my father's brother, came to the palace with his army and attacked us, taking my family hostage. He wants the crown and he will use the Rose to get it," I said, picking up the flower off the counter and stroking its soft petals.

"How will the Rose help him get the crown?" asked Darian, scratching his head in thought.

"The Rose possesses magical powers and it will allow him to go back into the past and change it." I hesitated before continuing. Darian deserved to know everything and I planned to hold nothing back from him.

"I know all of this because Gabriel told me. After I got the Rose, he held a dagger to my chest and threatened to kill me if I didn't give it to him…. Gabriel is working for Draxon."

I watched as Darian's face grew pale and then flushed red, his hands clenched into fists at his side. He jumped to his feet and kicked his stool across the room with a roar.

"I'm going to kill him," he growled, eyes flashing with rage.

"Darian, please calm down," I said, holding a hand up in the air.

"Is everything okay?" asked Thalia.

I jumped as she slid a plate of eggs and toast in front of me, wondering how long she had been standing there for, listening to our conversation.

"We're fine," I said, my voice trembling slightly as I looked over at Darian who was still fuming.

Thalia did not look entirely convinced but graciously retreated into the back room again where I had no doubt she would be listening to our entire conversation.

"I managed to get a hold of the dagger and I had him pinned against the wall." I felt a mix of sadness and anger that I couldn't describe rising inside of me as I recounted the events that were still very fresh and raw.

"I wanted to kill him so badly but I just couldn't bring myself to do it. So I left him there and told him that if he came after me again, I would not hesitate to kill him." My body began to shake uncontrollably and my teeth started to chatter.

Darian came over to me and wrapped his arms around me, holding me tightly against his chest. "It's okay now, Ari. He's gone. I won't ever let him hurt you again," he vowed.

I tried to steady my breathing, knowing he was right. "I'm sorry to dump all of this on you," I said, looking up into Darian's face. "I never wanted to be a burden to you."

"You are *not* a burden," he replied adamantly. "I made a choice to stay with you and see this through. And I mean it. I don't ever want you to feel like you can't tell me things."

A tear slipped down my cheek and I let it drip onto his shirt. I didn't deserve him. He had been there for me from the very beginning but I had walked away, thinking he was a liar who had only been using me.

I had run to the very person Darian had tried to protect me from and look where that had gotten me.

"We're going to do this, Ari," said Darian, determination set in the lines of his face and the crease of his brow. "Draxon is not going to win." He rested his hands on my back and his warm breath tickled my ear.

"You are in control. Draxon's only hope of victory is through you. And you aren't going to give that to him."

I let Darian's words linger in the air and I felt strangely comforted by his words. After a long moment, I reluctantly pulled away, not wanting to leave the safety of his arms. A newfound courage filled me, knowing that I wasn't in this alone.

"This is war," I said with fierce determination, grabbing the dagger off the counter and raising it in the air.

"Yes," Darian agreed, with a fiery glint in his eyes, "this is war."

Chapter 21

The harbour bustled with people despite the rain that continued to fall. The ships swayed back and forth at the dock and their sails flapped in the wind. Horse drawn carts splashed through puddles, making their way towards the docks carrying crates filled with supplies.

I held onto Darian's hand as we approached the docks, searching for the *Maryanne*. This was my one hope at getting back to Aurora. I could only hope the weather had prevented them from leaving port.

We had decided to leave the tavern right away so as not to delay things any longer. Every day that passed, I worried I would be too late to save my parents. Patience was not something Draxon had a lot of and I had no idea how long he would wait for me to return.

"Over there, at the far end," said Darian.

My eyes followed his hand as he pointed at a ship that was anchored at a dock at the far end of the harbour.

"Are you sure that's the *Maryanne*?" I asked, my breath catching in my throat.

"I would recognize that ship anywhere," Darian replied. "I know it inside and out."

I let Darian lead me through the bustling harbour, pulling me close to his side as a cart loaded with lumber splashed by us, shielding me from the muddy water that the horses kicked up.

I scanned the faces of the men who passed us, carrying boxes and crates or driving carts. I half expected to see Gabriel there among the crowd, looking for me. But I had warned him that if he came after me, I would kill him.

He had come after me before, but I knew he wouldn't this time. I had left him behind in the cave, and I didn't expect to see him again.

My heart skipped a beat and I attempted to swallow around the lump that had formed in my throat. As if sensing that something was wrong, Darian's eyes met mine and he gave my shoulder a comforting squeeze.

"One day, you will look back and this will all be behind you."

I blinked repeatedly as Darian's face grew blurry. "I hope so," I whispered.

I wanted to believe him but I wondered if Draxon would ever be part of my past. As long as he was alive, there was always the threat of him returning to usurp the throne or to threaten my life and the lives of my parents.

Darian fell silent as we approached the last dock. As much as I knew he wanted to reassure me that everything would work out for good, I knew he couldn't. Just like the horizon was clouded by mist and rain and you couldn't see across to the other side, there was no way of knowing what lay ahead or what the outcome of this situation would be.

"Darian? Ari?" came a sudden voice behind us. We both spun around to see Captain Carter, his brow furrowed with surprise.

"I didn't expect to see you two again after you left. What are you doing here?"

Darian looked at me, as if wondering what he should say.

"I caught up with Ari and we were able to get what she came for," he explained, quickly, not wanting to give too much information.

I could tell Captain Carter was confused by the situation and knew there was more going on than what we were saying but thankfully refrained from prying.

"We were hoping we could accompany you back to Aurora. I will gladly help the crew again but this will be my last voyage with you," said Darian.

I looked at him with confusion, not sure what he meant. *What was he planning to do after we got back to Aurora?*

Captain Carter nodded understandingly, his eyes lingering on our hands that were still clasped together. A small smile tugged at the corners of his mouth.

Heat traveled up my neck and into my cheeks at the implication. Everything was happening so fast, we hadn't even had time to discuss where we stood with each other or what would happen once this was all over. I couldn't think about the future or my own feelings and desires with so much at stake.

"You are more than welcome to travel on my ship back to Aurora. It would be my pleasure to have you both," Captain Carter said.

"Thank you so much," I said.

"Come and get out of the rain," said Captain Carter, gesturing towards the *Maryanne* where the sailors were continuing to load the remaining cargo. "As long as the weather continues to hold off, I would like to set sail tonight so we can be on our way. We have already been delayed a few days waiting for the repairs to be done. We're lucky that more damage wasn't done to the ship."

"Well, we're thankful for the slight delay, Cap'n," chuckled Darian. "We were worried we would have to wait to find another ship back to Aurora. It seems we caught you just in time."

"That you did," said Captain Carter.

We boarded the ship out of the wind and cold drizzling rain that continued to fall.

"I suggest you two go and see if you can scrounge up something to eat and find some dry clothes to wear. I'm sure some of the other sailors have some extra clothes you can wear."

I nodded gratefully, following Darian below deck as Captain Carter made his way towards his office to get things in order for the voyage.

"I'm sure we look terrible," I said with a laugh, looking at Darian's wet, mud-stained clothes that clung to his body and his blonde hair which stuck up in all directions.

Darian's laughter echoed my own as he took in my own disheveled appearance. He brushed a wet strand of hair out of my eyes and brushed a clump of mud off my shirt.

As I followed Darian into the men's sleeping quarters, a small room lined with bunk beds, I couldn't help but think about how much had changed in the few days since I had been on the *Maryanne*. It felt like it had been weeks ago that we were on this ship together.

Darian lifted the lid of a wooden chest which contained extra pants and shirts. He held up a few, trying to find the smallest ones.

"I think these will do," he said, handing me a white shirt and a pair of beige pants. "You might need to use some rope to hold the pants up," he said with a smirk.

"I'm sure I can make them work," I said with a laugh. "I'll be so glad to put on dry clothes again."

Darian pulled out a shirt and a pair of pants for himself.

"I'll go change upstairs and then meet you in the kitchen," I said, making my way towards the door.

"Sounds good," said Darian. "I'm starving."

I made my way upstairs to the closet beside the Captain's room that had been my sleeping quarters on the voyage to Destin. I walked into the small room to see my cot still there and made up with blankets, as if I had never left.

I shut the door and quickly changed into the clothes Darian had given me. They were a little baggy but surprisingly fit quite well. I ran my fingers through my wet hair and tried to make myself look somewhat presentable.

My mother was always chiding me on my appearance, claiming that I always had dirt on my clothes from riding Marquis. I had never been the lady-like daughter I'm sure she had wished I would be. She would probably have a fit if she could see what I was wearing right now.

A small tear slid down my cheek as I wished I could see her right now and know that she was alive.

In a little over a week, I would be back in Aurora. I had no idea what I would do once I got there. All I could do was wait and hope we would get there in time.

These same thoughts filled my mind later that night as I watched the shore slip away and the horizon loom before us as the *Maryanne* set sail again.

The cool wind blew my hair into my eyes and I could feel Darian's comforting hand on my back as we stood at the railing, watching the churning waves splash against the side of the ship.

There was nothing more I could do except wait for the day to come when I would face Draxon and defeat him once and for all. Wait for the day when I could return to fight for my country, my kingdom and my family. I could only hope and pray that there would be something left to fight for.

Chapter 22

The sails flapped in the wind and the brisk sea air stung my face as I leaned over the edge of the railing, watching the hull cut through the waves. I could see the town of Aurora slowly taking shape before my eyes as we approached shore. No longer a green blob on the horizon, I could make out the steepled tops of stone buildings which rose above the treeline. I could see what looked like white clouds dotting the shoreline, the other merchant ships anchored in the harbour, waiting to set sail or returning from a voyage.

I looked over my shoulder to see another ship sailing alongside us, cutting through the waves with precision and anticipation of setting foot on land again after more than a week at sea. While we had left Aurora alone, another ship had accompanied us from Destin with a large shipment of flour, sugar and oatmeal.

I ran my hand absently along the railing, my heart skipping a beat when my fingers brushed against someone else's. I looked up and my eyes met Darian's sheepish ones.

"How does it feel to be home?" he asked, gently, intertwining his fingers with mine.

I let out a deep breath and fixed my gaze on the port. "Terrifying," I answered honestly, feeling my heart skip a beat again.

A gentle breeze ruffled my hair, blowing some loose strands into my eyes. I tucked them behind my ear, like my mother always did when I was younger after I had been outside playing.

"It's one thing to imagine what is going to happen when you come back and to plan what to say to Draxon. But it's a completely different thing when that moment actually comes and you have to face the reality of the situation. I don't even know if my parents are still alive….." My voice trailed off, turning into a sob. My shoulders shook as the tears burned the backs of my eyes, slowly trickling down my cheeks.

I let go of Darian's hand and fell into his arms, pressing my face into his broad shoulders. The scent of salt and ocean breeze clung to his clothes and the warm rays of sunshine beat down on my back.

We stood there in silence, swaying together in rhythm with the ship, rocking against the waves. There was nothing to say. Lies wouldn't comfort me and neither would the truth. I had no idea what awaited me at the palace. My *home*.

The home that no longer felt like a safe place because it had been taken over by a monster. A monster who held my parents in chains, like criminals.

I would make him pay for every amount of suffering he had inflicted on my parents.

"Ready the sails!" came Captain Carter's bellowing voice, carried on the wind.

I pulled away from Darian as the sailors filled the deck, scrambling around, preparing the ship for docking.

I stepped to the side as Darian went to join the fray, watching the scene before me. It was as if I was watching from above, like a fly on the wall, powerless to do anything to change what was happening. I had felt this way many times over the past few weeks, like I was watching my life spiral out of control, unable to change the course I had been set upon.

The die had been cast, the cards dealt. The play was in motion and the only thing I could do was go along with the game and try not to lose everything.

Stepping onto land felt foreign after almost two weeks at sea. I instantly missed the rocking of the ship beneath me. I could see how some people dedicated their life to sailing around the ocean, traveling from port to port and never dropping anchor for too long. There was a tiny piece of me that wished I could hop back on the *Maryanne* and set sail again and leave all my problems behind me.

But I knew I could only run for so long. The title *princess* would always follow me and my crown would always call me home. Those who have a kingdom on their shoulders don't have the luxury of running from their problems.

I would be loyal to my parents and to my country, even if it cost me my life.

"I will be sad to see you go, Ari," said Captain Carter, coming up alongside me on the dock.

"Thank you for everything you have done for me," I said sincerely, hoping the Captain could see my appreciation.

"It has been my pleasure to have you accompany my crew on this voyage." He extended a worn, wind-weathered hand to me and I shook it gratefully.

"If you ever need to cross the ocean again, you will always have a place on the *Maryanne*," Captain Carter said.

"I might take you up on that offer one day," I said with a smile.

"I hope you do," he replied, with a tip of his cap. I watched as he walked away to direct the sailors who were unloading the cargo, shouting commands in his now familiar, booming voice.

I wasn't sure if my path would cross with Captain Carter or his crew again but I was glad they had for a short time.

Darian approached me, carrying two wooden crates stacked on top of each other. "I have arranged for a friend of mine to take us close to the palace. We can walk the rest of the way so we don't raise any suspicion," he said in a lowered voice, his eyes flitting around the bustling wharf to make sure no one was listening.

"Thank you," I said, my stomach churning with unease.

Darian walked away to finish unloading, leaving me to contemplate the *what ifs* and worst case scenarios alone.

In a few short hours, we would be at the palace and I would have to face Draxon. I still didn't have a plan but I knew that I couldn't give the Rose to Draxon. I wasn't willing to stake my life on his word.

The sun was still high in the sky when we left the harbour, squished in a rickety horse-drawn cart beside a plump man with a receding hairline and a grey beard that touched the top of his chest. We sat in silence most of the drive, getting tossed around after every bump we crossed over. Finally, we reached a long, winding road that split in two, one leading down to a few houses owned by noblemen and another that led up to the palace.

"Thank you for your service," said Darian, "and for your discretion." He handed the man a leather pouch that jingled with coins.

"My pleasure," he said, his eyes widening as he accepted it.

Darian took my hand as I jumped down from the wagon and we stood at the side of the road. The man spurred his two black mares with a slap of the reins against their broad flanks, kicking up a cloud of dust as they drove away.

We stood in silence, watching until the wagon was out of sight. Then, Darian turned to me, his eyes flecked with worry. "It's time."

I forced my feet to move, one step after another, bringing me closer to the palace, to Draxon and to my parents.

Before I knew it, the palace gates loomed before me and my stomach twisted into a ball of knots. A wave of nausea swept over me and I felt Darian give my hand a reassuring squeeze. I had waited for this moment when I could return home with the Rose but now that it was here, fear gripped my heart and I had no idea what to say or do.

Should I stand up to Draxon and refuse to give him the Rose? Or should I give it to him and demand that he leave my family and our people alone?

What would Draxon do once he had the Rose in his hands?

I could see the worry in Darian's eyes as he watched me, unsure what he could say that would comfort me.

My heart skipped a beat as I saw two guards approaching the gate, their hands resting on the hilts of their swords which glittered in the sunlight.

"Who are you?" demanded the taller of the two men, his dark brown eyes studying us suspiciously.

"You can tell Draxon that Princess Arianna has returned," I said, fighting against the tremor that threatened to fill my voice. I stood up straighter and locked eyes with first one guard and then the other.

The two guards exchanged a glance, their eyebrows raised with surprise. They probably hadn't expected me to return. I wonder if Draxon had thought the same.

"Who is your companion?" asked the other guard, taking a step closer to the gate to get a better look at Darian.

I opened my mouth to speak but Darian spoke first. "I'm Darian and wherever the princess goes, I will be going too," he said firmly, leaving no room for debate.

I glanced at Darian as the guards mumbled quietly among themselves.

My heart skipped a beat as one of the men produced a large metal key which hung from a loop on his pants. The grinding of the key in the lock set my teeth on edge and I could hear the blood pounding in my ears as the gate swung open. I doubted the gate had been opened since I left what felt like an eternity ago.

One of the guards grabbed my arm roughly while the other seized Darian.

"Let go of us," exclaimed Darian, his green eyes flashing angrily.

I stayed silent, knowing I would need to save what energy I had left. I suddenly felt tired. Tired of running, of searching, of worrying, of being afraid. Tired of fighting for something I might end up losing no matter what I did.

The guards dragged us into the palace as Darian continued to struggle against their hold on him.

I felt my heart thud dully in my chest, in unison with the heavy oak door that was shut and bolted behind us. I blinked, trying to adjust to the dim lighting inside. The drapes were drawn across all the windows, blocking out any rays of sunlight that attempted to peek through. The palace was eerily quiet, the only sound Darian's heavy breathing beside me as he gave up his futile struggle.

A guard rounded the corner, sword drawn and brow furrowed in confusion.

"Tell His Highness that the girl has returned and brought a companion with her," barked the guard holding me.

My blood began to boil inside of me, thrumming inside my eardrums and coursing through my veins. "That *monster*," I spat, "will never bear that title in this kingdom or wear my father's crown."

The man holding me tilted his head back and let out a deep bellow of laughter that rang off the cold stone surrounding us. "He already is."

A chill ran through my body and the room began to spin. My heart raced as the implication of his words became clear.

No. No, no, no, no. I repeated the words over and over in my mind until they became audible.

"No. No, no, no!" My voice rose in pitch and hysteria until I was screaming, flailing my body around in desperation, kicking, punching and biting the guard, trying to break free. The only thing that mattered was finding my parents. They were alive, they had to be.

Out of the corner of my eye, I saw the guard who had gone to let Draxon know of our arrival return and beckon for us to follow.

I dug my feet into the cracks in between the stone tiles, dragging my feet against the floor. I couldn't face the man who had murdered my family. Not now, not ever.

My attempts did nothing to slow down the guard who held me. His grip around my arms tightened and he dug his nails into my skin. I ignored the stinging pain and the tingling sensation that crept into my hands, growing more panicked as we approached the throne room.

I saw the double doors open ahead of me, like the yawning mouth of a dark cavern, threatening to swallow me whole. It was like walking into a den of wolves with a blindfold on. You already knew you wouldn't come out alive.

Chapter 23

"Arianna, we meet again," came Draxon's familiar sneer.

I stopped struggling at the sound of his menacing voice. I saw a faint flicker as one candle was lit and then another. I blinked, letting my eyes adjust to the light.

My eyes landed on Draxon, seated on my father's throne, the light reflecting off of his bejeweled crown bearing the Oberian royal crest. Two swords crossed over a shield with a wolf in the middle.

"How dare you sit there and pretend to be a king?" I growled, clenching my hands into fists at my side, letting my nails dig into my palms.

"Pretend?" said Draxon with a chuckle. "Why should one pretend to have something that is already theirs?"

Fury bleeding from my pores, I lunged towards him but the guard wrenched me back throwing me to the ground. I smashed my head off the stone, a sharp pain bursting through me.

"What are you talking about?" I asked through gritted teeth, lifting my head to meet Draxon's glittering eyes.

Ignoring my question, Draxon let his hand glide along the side of the black marble throne, encased in jewels. "I underestimated you, Arianna," he said.

I picked myself up off the floor and raised myself to my full height. I walked towards my father's throne, my footsteps echoing off the stone in the silent room.

One of the guards grabbed my arm in his vise-like grip, but Draxon motioned for him to let me go.

I stopped in front of Draxon, looking into his dark, beady eyes.

"I did not expect you to come back alive you know," he stated.

"I know," I said, narrowing my eyes at Draxon's words. Unease swept over me, making the hairs on my arms and the back of my neck stand on end.

"Smart girl." He paused, looking me up and down, structinizing me. "So where is the Rose?" Draxon asked, his hands grasping greedily at the air, as if seeing the Rose before him in his mind's eye.

Darian had given me another backpack he had found on the ship so I wouldn't have to risk carrying the Rose around in public. I wasn't ready to reveal that card to Draxon yet.

"I want to see my parents," I said, planting my feet firmly. "If you release them, I will give you what you want."

"No, Ari, don't trust him," exclaimed Darian, causing me to whirl around in his direction. I had forgotten he was still in the room. A single guard with a mop of dark hair, who didn't look to be much older than us, still held him captive.

"Who is your friend?" asked Draxon, a hint of mischief entering his voice. My heart skipped a beat as I watched Draxon's hawk-like eyes land on Darian.

"We met on my journey," I said, not wishing to disclose any information about Darian that could be used against him.

I cast a sidelong glance at Darian, wordlessly telling him to keep quiet. Darian's face had grown pale and his green eyes were filled with worry.

Draxon watched our exchange with growing curiosity, as I shifted nervously from foot to foot.

"Bring my parents to me immediately," I commanded, turning to face the guards who stood behind me, ready to grab me at any moment should I attempt to lunge at Draxon again.

Draxon cackled with delight at my stern voice, ordering his guards around. "You forget *princess*," he mocked, "I'm the one who is in charge around here. My men do not take their orders from you."

Heat crawled up my neck and into my cheeks as anger slowly rose inside of me.

"We had a deal, Draxon. I would get you the Rose if you released my parents, alive and unharmed. I have done my part, now it's your turn to do yours," I demanded, crossing my arms defiantly.

A dark scowl passed over his face and his eyes flashed angrily. With a flick of his wrist, he beckoned to one of the guards to open the doors that led into the throne room.

My breath caught in my throat as my parents were led into the room in chains. My father's left eye was black with bruises and he looked like he had lost twenty pounds or more. My mother's skin looked sallow and sickly and her eyes were sunk in with dark shadows under her eyes. They did not look like the king and queen I had left behind. My parents had been reduced to prisoners at Draxon's disposal to do with as he wished.

"Ari!" exclaimed my mother with what little energy she could muster. It was as if a dim light had been lit in her eyes as they sparked faintly to life.

My father squinted his one good eye, trying to make out my figure in the darkness. His mouth widened in surprise, like he couldn't believe I was actually there in the flesh.

"I'm back," I said, not sure what else to say. I wanted to run to them but I worried what the guards would do to them, or to me, if I did.

"Release them to me at once," I ordered firmly, this time directing my command to Draxon. "I will give you what you want."

"Don't Ari," protested my father. "You cannot give him the Rose. He will destroy our kingdom if you do."

My gaze flitted from my father's pleading gaze back to Draxon's gleeful face.

"You do like to strike a fair deal, don't you princess?" He cackled. "Unfortunately, I'm not as foolish as you might think I am. I have not seen proof that you even have the Rose. Where is it?"

I hesitated before sliding my backpack off my shoulder and placing it on the floor with a thud. I slowly opened it up, peering inside to see the Rose lying on top of my dagger, a faint red glow pulsing from its petals.

I grasped it in my clammy hand, pulling it slowly from the bag and holding it up for all to see. I watched Draxon's narrowed eyes glitter greedily.

"You have your proof," I said, "now release my parents," I ground out between gritted teeth. I was tired of Draxon's games and I was determined to stand my ground.

The guards holding my parents cast questioning glances at Draxon, unsure what to do.

"Release them," said Draxon, after a moment's thought, his eyes fixed on the Rose. The prospect of power was more alluring than his revenge against my father.

My heart pounded in my chest as the guards undid my parents chains, letting them fall to the ground with a clatter.

My mother fell to her knees on the cold marble floor, tears of joy and relief spilling down her cheeks. My father stood in disbelief, turning his hands over and over where the chains used to be.

I took a step towards the throne, realizing I had no other choice but to trust Draxon. He had kept his word to release my parents and now I had to give him the Rose. My eyes flitted to the doors, already knowing they were heavily guarded.

The tension in the room was like the moment of calm before a storm, the dark clouds racing across the sky, towards you.

I took another slow step towards the throne, eyeing Draxon's bony hand, covered in ruby, emerald and sapphire rings. A reminder of who had the power, of who had the upper hand.

My parents and Darian were silent, knowing there was nothing they could say to convince me, even if I did have the option to change my mind.

I had walked into this room knowing full well that I was walking into a trap. This was Draxon's territory. He controlled the pawns and the cards, dealing what he wished to each person. We had no choice but to accept what we had been dealt.

The card of surrender was heavy in my hand, and the taste of defeat was bitter in my mouth.

I stretched out my hand towards Draxon, ready to give him the Rose.

Suddenly, the doors to the throne room burst open.

"Stop!" came a frantic cry, as a boy with a mop of dark curly hair tumbled into the room, a group of guards right on his heels.

"We're terribly sorry, Your Highness," sputtered a trembling guard, the end of his greying beard quivering as he spoke. "The lad somehow got past the guards at the gate and—"

"Bring him here," ordered Draxon, a dark shadow passing over his face.

Stunned, the guards obeyed, dragging the struggling boy towards the throne.

The boy lifted his head and our eyes met. My breath caught in my throat and my heart stopped. Time stood still as I looked into the eyes of the boy I had thought I would never see again.

"Don't give him the Rose," said Gabriel, his voice breathy and hoarse.

My head spun and dark spots filled my vision. *What was Gabriel doing here? How had he followed me all the way from Destin?* Hundreds of questions whirled through my brain, each going unanswered.

I blinked, steadying my racing heart and watching to see what would happen next. Fear gripped me as I saw Draxon's eyes narrow like a lion watching its prey before it pounced.

"You traitor," growled Draxon, reaching out a claw-like hand to grab Gabriel around the neck. The guards let go, giving him up to be devoured by a monster.

"And you are a liar," choked out Gabriel, Draxon's hand relaxing slightly to allow him to speak.

"You had one job," barked Draxon, "and you couldn't even do it."

"I couldn't kill someone I knew was innocent," Gabriel replied.

Draxon gave Gabriel a rough shove towards me, causing him to stumble.

"What are you doing here?" I asked, breathlessly, my stomach churning. "Didn't my threat mean anything to you?" I desperately wanted to be angry with him but I couldn't.

The tiniest smirk played at the corners of Gabriel's lips. "It would be hard to kill me if you were already dead."

I choked on a laugh that threatened to spill from my lips. "You have a morbid sense of humour."

A dark cackle filled the room, echoing off the stone and ringing in my ears.

"Well, isn't this quite the turn of events," mused Draxon, his eyes landing on Gabriel. "You are in love with her," he accused.

"How do you feel about that, Stephen," he asked, his gaze turning to my father who had his arm wrapped tightly around my mother. "A perfect match, I'd say," he smirked. "The traitor's daughter marries the boy who almost killed her for a few gold coins."

His cackle rang out in the silent room.

"And I still have no idea who this boy is," Draxon said, gesturing to Darian, "but I would assume he's in love with her too."

"Young and foolish love," he said, getting up from the throne and beginning to pace around the platform, his eyes taking on a faraway look.

"I was in love once, to a duke's daughter who thought less of me than a bug beneath her shoe. She chose one of my own guards over me, a prince who could give her everything she could ever dream of and more."

Draxon paused, letting his hollow eyes meet Gabriel's and then Darian's. "Do you really think she loves either of you? She has played with you both, used you to help her and save her own life. I bet she made you each think you could have a future with her once this is all over. She will never choose either of you, that much I can promise."

A flame of rage was lit inside of me, threatening to burn anyone in sight.

"How dare you say that?!" I exclaimed furiously, raising myself up to my full height and approaching Draxon. "Don't pretend to know me or my heart."

Draxon appeared totally unphased by my words. "I'll let you deal with your little love triangle in a minute," sneered Draxon. "Just give me the Rose."

I looked from Draxon to my parents, to Gabriel, to Darian, to all the guards surrounding us, their hands on the hilt of their swords, ready to draw them at Draxon's command.

I realized at that moment how many people he had manipulated, how many people he had spoon-fed lies, made to appear as truth. I was naive to believe that I would truly be free from Draxon and his games once he had the Rose.

He wanted me to believe that once he had the Rose, he would leave my family alone. But that would only be the beginning. If Draxon had the Rose, we would always be his puppets on strings.

"Never," I said, looking Draxon square in the face. "You never intended to let me live, or my family. If Gabriel had succeeded in killing me and returned with the Rose, you would have killed my parents and taken over the throne. You were never going to keep your word, were you?" It was a statement not a question and I saw in Draxon's eyes that it was true.

With a flash of metal, Draxon drew the sword at his waist and thrust the point against my neck.

"You think you're so smart, figuring out the bad guy's plans and trying to be the hero. But all you are is delusional, believing that you have any chance of winning. Look around! My guards are everywhere, ready to kill everyone in this room at my command. It's time to stop playing games and accept the reality of the situation. Give me the Rose or else…." His voice trailed off and he snapped his fingers in the air with his free hand.

Immediately, the guards drew their swords and ran towards my parents, pointing the blades at their throats. "Your parents will be the first to die."

My heart hammered in my chest and I couldn't swallow around the lump that had formed in my throat. I reached out my hand towards Draxon again, still clutching tightly to the Rose. I was surrendering my life, my kingdom and my crown to a monster.

Suddenly, the two guards who held my parents drew their swords and let out a deafening shout. The doors to the throne room burst open and a crowd of men wielding swords, pitchforks and axes poured into the room, like an army of ants.

Draxon's dark eyes widened and fear flashed across his face, letting the blade he held against my neck fall helplessly to his side.

"Run!" screamed my father above the deafening sound of metal on metal.

I had no idea what was happening but I did as I was told. I ran.

Chapter 24

Blood thundered in my ears as I raced down the dark and twisted corridor, hair trailing behind me. The palace was under attack. That was obvious. *But by who?* Based on Draxon's fear, I assumed they weren't on his side. *But if they weren't his men, whose were they?*

"Ari!"

My name rang down the hallway. Heart pounding, I stopped abruptly in my tracks and whirled around to see who was following me.

Gabriel ran towards me, breathing heavily. "Ari, I need to talk to you."

"Now is really not the time," I said, gesturing a hand in the direction of the throne room, as if I needed to remind him that our lives were at stake.

"I know, I know but please, this is important." His green eyes were glassy and pleading.

I let out a breath and folded my arms over my chest. Gabriel took that as an indication to speak.

"When you found the Rose in the cave, I knew what I had to do. Draxon wanted me to kill you and bring him the Rose. I thought that the money would help to get me off the streets so I could start a better life for myself. But I realized that you weren't the enemy. Draxon was. And I couldn't kill you because...." His breath caught in his throat and I watched his throat bob as he tried to swallow around the lump in his throat.

"I love you, Ari. I know I have broken your trust and hurt you but I want you to know that I'm not giving up on you. On *us*."

I blinked furiously as Gabriel's face blurred before my eyes. "Gabriel I—" My sentence was interrupted as the doors to the throne room burst open and Darian entered the hallway.

"Ari! Is everything okay?" Darian froze as he caught sight of Gabriel at my side.

"Yes, but we need to get out of here before someone finds us. Let's go." I began to run down the hallway towards the door that I knew led into the back courtyard by the stables.

"They're our friends, Ari. A bunch of the guards and villagers led a revolt and somehow managed to infiltrate the palace. Most of Draxon's men are dead but no one has seen Draxon. He disappeared and it's only a matter of time before he comes looking for you."

Simultaneous relief and fear filled me. *Saved.* But victory was not ours if Draxon had escaped.

"I have to find him," I said with determination.

"Are you crazy, Ari? He will kill you! You have to run," exclaimed Gabriel, grabbing my arm.

I jerked it away roughly and took a step down the hallway. "I need to do this," I said, "or else I will never truly be free of Draxon."

Darian and Gabriel exchanged a glance, letting their gaze settle on me.

"Take this," said Darian, handing me a sword that he had clutched at his side. It felt heavy and cold in my hand.

"What will you do?" I asked.

"I'm going back in to help where I'm needed. I'll make sure your parents are safe," said Darian.

"Thank you," I murmured, trying not to let the worry seep into my voice.

"Let me come with you," demanded Gabriel.

"No, I'm going alone," I said, firmly. "Go help Darian with whatever is needed. I'll be fine."

I turned my back on them and began to run down the hallway, sword gripped tightly at my side.

I didn't look behind me. I knew this was what I needed to do. For my parents, for my people, for myself. I was not going to let Draxon get away with this. I had vowed when I left the cave that I would kill Draxon.

And I would keep my promise.

It didn't take long to find Draxon. I knew the palace like the back of my hand but I knew the forests better. He had fled on foot but I was much faster on Marquis who must have wandered back to the palace after I had left on my journey.

Marquis stopped in his tracks as I jumped to the ground, sword drawn and ready. I had watched the guards practice enough times to know what to do.

A wicked grin spread across Draxon's face as he watched me standing there with my sword. "Just like a little girl playing pretend," he snickered.

He drew his own sword, the metal glinting in the waning sunlight.

"You don't want to do this, Arianna."

"The tables have turned Draxon," I stated, coldly. "I have been given a new hand but I think you're out of cards. What are you going to do?" I took a step closer to him and then another. "Where are you going to run?"

It wasn't a question, it was a threat, and Draxon knew it too.

"Give me the Rose, Arianna," he said, eyes flashing angrily.

I could hear the desperation in his voice.

I thrust my sword towards him as he raised his. They met with the screeching clash of metal on metal.

"Put down your sword, before you get hurt, *princess*."

"I'm not afraid to bleed," I retorted, thrusting my sword towards his exposed abdomen. Draxon looked ridiculous in his long, flowing black robe, his fingers still covered in my father's stolen rings.

Draxon blocked my move with his sword, the sound of the clashing blades sending a flock of birds scattering from the trees into the sky.

"Why do you want the Rose so much?" I asked, watching the tip of Draxon's sword warily as we sparred again.

"You wouldn't understand," he said with a bitter laugh. "The girl who has been raised with everything a person could ever dream of doesn't know what it means to have nothing."

"I may have been raised with privilege, but I have seen my parents sacrifice on a daily basis for our people."

Draxon spun around, trying to twist my sword out of my grasp but I leapt backwards out of his reach.

"The Rose might give you power, but it won't bring you happiness," I said. "You think once you have the Rose, you can use the magic to have the life you've always wanted but you're the one who is delusional," I said, feeling the tiniest twinge of pity for him.

Draxon angrily charged at me but I stood my ground, raising my sword to meet his. Neither of us had an advantage and appeared to be equally matched. But the battle had to end sometime and I was determined that I would be the one left standing.

My mind whirled with ideas, trying to think of how I could get Draxon to surrender. We were on the edge of the forest, near a towering cliff that overlooked the village and the farms that filled the valley.

I thrust my sword towards Draxon's chest, catching him off guard and tearing a bit of the fabric away. Just enough to startle him, but not enough to draw blood.

I tore off for the cliff, clutching my sword at my side. I heard Draxon's running footsteps crunching on the leaves and fallen branches that covered the forest floor.

I leapt agilely over a fallen log, weaving around trees, trying to put as much distance between us as I could. I knew Draxon would catch up eventually, but I needed to get a head start. All my years of playing in the forests was finally paying off.

I reached the cliff, sucking in a deep breath of air as I surveyed the homes below that looked like brown specks on a green canvas. I could hear Draxon crashing through the bushes with an infuriated roar, and I knew I needed to act fast.

Throwing my backpack carelessly to the ground, I undid the clasp that held it closed and took out the Rose. A shooting pain ran through my arm and I could feel the mark on my arm burning. I bit my lip to stifle a cry and positioned myself on the edge of the cliff, holding the Rose in one hand and my sword in the other.

A split second later, Draxon emerged through the trees panting and red in the face. The colour quickly drained from his face when he saw me dangling the Rose over the edge of the cliff.

"Don't do anything foolish, Arianna," he said, slowly making his way towards me.

"Come any closer and I will," I said, threateningly.

"You wouldn't dare."

I let my fingers loosen around the stem, dangling it closer to the edge of the cliff.

I watched with satisfaction as Draxon's knuckles turned white as he gripped his sword.

I had the upper hand now and there was no denying it.

"I will make you pay for what you have done. You don't deserve forgiveness."

"Maybe not," said Draxon with a smirk, "but isn't that the right thing to do?" He mocked.

"All my life I have done the right thing, sacrificed what I wanted for my family and my people. I've forgiven people who have hurt me and betrayed me. But not anymore. I'm done with your games, Draxon. This time, I win."

I let the Rose fall.

In that moment, it was as if time stood still. It was over. A weight lifted off my chest and I felt like I could breathe for the first time as I watched the Rose flutter over the edge of the cliff. It landed on the rocks far below, sending up a flare of red light before growing dark.

Immediately, a shooting pain burst through my arm. I collapsed to the ground, black spots dancing at the edge of my vision.

"What have you done?" roared Draxon.

Out of the corner of my eyes, I saw him bar his sword and charge at me where I was hunched over on the ground.

Was this how it would end? Had I gotten rid of the Rose, only to die anyways?

I saw the glint of metal as the tip of the blade drew closer.

Then, Draxon collapsed on the ground as someone tackled him from behind.

"Gabriel?" I choked out, with astonishment.

He held the blade of his sword against Draxon's throat, ready to slit it at any moment.

"This is not your fight," growled Draxon breathlessly.

I cried out as another searing pain tore through my body and the mark on my arm began to glow bright red.

Gabriel's gaze darted to me and he relaxed his grip slightly on his sword. Seeing his chance, Draxon ducked out of Gabriel's hold, grabbing his own sword from the ground in front of him and leaping to his feet.

Gabriel met Draxon's sword in the air and they stood eye to eye, blade to blade.

My heart raced frantically as I watched the exchange, powerless to do anything. I grabbed my sword from beside me and tried to get to my feet. My head began to spin and I felt nauseous from the pain, too weak to stand.

Gabriel was the first to let his sword down, thrusting it just below Draxon's shoulder blade. The tip of his sword grazed Draxon's face, cutting a thin line across his cheek. Red began to seep from the cut and ran down his skin.

Draxon's lower lip curled into an ugly sneer as he blocked Gabriel's thrust. He jutted his sword towards Gabriel's neck, causing him to stumble backwards, but not lose his balance.

My breath caught in my throat, not knowing what was going to happen. Draxon had murder in his eyes and I knew only one of them would walk away from the fight.

I curled over on the ground as another wave of pain washed over me. I didn't know what was happening to me. Maybe if the Rose died, the *Keeper* did too.

My head pounded with the sound of their blades clashing above me. I could smell sweat and blood as they sparred, neither gaining an advantage over their opponent.

I grabbed my sword, trying to muster the strength to lift it. I could see the exhaustion on Gabriel's face and I wasn't sure how much longer he would last.

I got to my knees and then to my feet, wobbling unsteadily. I pressed a clammy hand against my temple, trying to stop the spinning.

Suddenly, Draxon knocked Gabriel's sword out of his hand, sending it flying to the ground a few feet away. Gabriel froze and his green eyes filled with fear. Without hesitation, Draxon plunged his sword into Gabriel's chest.

I screamed and ran towards them, my sword stretched out in front of me. Draxon whirled around and I ran my sword through his abdomen. A wracking sob tore through my body and collapsed to my knees beside Gabriel.

He had fallen to the ground, Draxon's sword still jutting out of his chest. Blood poured from the wound, staining his shirt. Sweat lined his brow and his upper lip and his eyes had a distant look in them.

"Gabriel, Gabriel, Gabriel," I repeated, tears streaming down my cheeks and falling onto his blood stained shirt.

I clutched his hand in mine, shutting out the sounds of Draxon coughing and gasping for air behind me.

Dusk had fallen and death hung thick in the air around us.

"You saved me," I whispered, my voice choked with tears.

Gabriel slowly turned his face towards mine, the tiniest smile toying at his lips. "You saved yourself."

My shoulders shook as I rested a trembling hand on Gabriel's flushed cheek.

"I need you," I cried.

A small tear trickled from Gabriel's eye and slid down his cheek.

"You don't need me. You saved your family and your kingdom all on your own. I'm thankful that I got to see you do it." His words came slowly, barely audible but I clung to each one.

"I'll get Marquis and take you back to the palace. The doctors will help you," I explained in a rush of words.

Gabriel gave my hand a gentle squeeze. "Please, stay with me."

Another sob tore through my body and I laid my head on his chest. It continued to rise and fall as his heartbeat slowed.

"We've already said too many goodbyes," I whispered.

I felt Gabriel's hand stroke my hair, wrapping a stray strand around his fingers. "Just goodbye for a little while," he mumbled, his breathing growing shallow.

A wracking cough tore through his body and I lifted my head off his chest. His green eyes were wide as he struggled to breathe in one raspy breath after another. He coughed again but this time, no air came from his lips.

He struggled for another breath as a shudder ran through him. My vision blurred as his eyelids fluttered closed. They didn't open again.

Chapter 25

I awoke to the sound of my name, echoing through the forest. Night had fallen and the moon cast shadows on the ground, illuminating Gabriel's lifeless form beside me. I sat up, rubbing my eyes that were sore and swollen from crying, not willing to believe that Gabriel was actually gone.

I held my hand over his lips, praying that I would feel his warm breath but there was nothing.

"Arianna!" came another cry, echoing through the trees.

I saw torchlight through the trees and heard the sound of horses' hooves crunching on dead leaves.

Suddenly, I saw Darian's comforting face as he entered the clearing, mounted on a black horse bearing the palace's royal insignia.

"I found her," he called to the rest of the search party.

Darian leapt off his horse and ran to my side, kneeling beside Gabriel's body and wrapping his arms around me. I laid my head against his shoulder and let the tears fall.

"What happened?" he asked gently, running a hand through my hair and pressing a kiss on my forehead.

I pulled away from him to gesture to Draxon's body behind me, the sword protruding from his chest, glinting in the moonlight.

Darian nodded solemnly and pulled me close to him again. Sobs shook my body as the guards entered the scene and began removing the bodies.

Darian picked me up in my arms and carried me over to his horse, not wanting me to see anymore than I already had.

"Your parents are waiting back at the palace for you," he murmured.

I wiped the tears from my eyes and smoothed my ruffled hair as Darian climbed up on the horse with me. I wrapped my arms around his waist, letting my eyes linger on the clearing one last time.

The guards were merely shadows in the darkness, taking away the dead. Taking away the boy with the hazel eyes and curly hair. The boy who always had a twinkle in his eyes and a smirk on his face.

The boy I had loved.

My parents were pacing the palace courtyard when Darian and I returned. I leapt off the horse and ran into my parents waiting arms, the arms I had thought would never hug me again.

I could taste salt on my lips and feel my parents' tears dripping into my hair. I felt my mother squeezing my hand in hers and my father's rubbing my back.

I shut my eyes tightly, not wanting to open them for fear that if I did, this would all be just an illusion and my parents would be gone again.

After a moment that ended far too soon, we pulled away but my mother did not let go of my hand.

Darian stood awkwardly to the side, watching our emotional reunion. My father walked over to him and wrapped him in a hug.

"Thank you for bringing our daughter back to us," he whispered.

"It was my honour," Darian replied, glancing over at me with a soft smile.

"We have lots to discuss," my father said, straightening his shoulders and resuming the position of a king.

"Nothing that can't wait for the morning," said my mother gently.

We entered the palace, the place that I had once called home. Torches had been lit to chase away the darkness but I still felt Draxon's presence. I saw his shadow in the corridor, felt his guards around every corner. Death hung thick in the air and I couldn't chase away the sight of bodies fallen on the cold marble floors.

A shiver ran down my spine and I felt Darian's comforting hand on my shoulder, reminding me that everything was okay now. But even though Draxon was dead, the battle fought and won, nothing would be the same again.

"One of the guards managed to escape when Draxon attacked," my father explained, his voice echoing in the empty room. "He was in hiding for a few weeks and then he was able to rally together many of the villagers to attack the palace."

I nodded, not wanting to consider what would have happened if they hadn't attacked when they did. I probably would not be standing in the palace with my parents, alive and safe.

So many lives had been lost, sacrificed for my family and the crown. A high price to pay. I thought of Gabriel who had returned and died a hero, even though he had once been on the side of the enemy. I wished I could have thanked him. Apologized for all the times I had hurt him. Told him I loved him.

But none of that mattered now. There was no going back or changing what had happened. Life would go on. My parents would resume their royal duties. I would finish my schooling and prepare to be the queen I had been born to be.

One day, Draxon and all that had happened would be just a memory, a story I would tell my children and my grandchildren. A story that involved a girl who didn't want to be a princess, two boys who wanted a new life and an adventure, a power-hungry monster, and a Red Rose.

A few days later, I stood on the dock overlooking the Aquarian sea, the rising sun a fiery ball on the horizon. I could feel the salty spray on my face, the wind in my hair and Darian's hand in mine.

I looked over at him with a smile, watching his twinkling green eyes sparkle in the sunlight.

"I can hear the sea calling my name," he said, softly.

"I hear it too," I said.

The *Maryanne* was anchored at the docks, her billowing white sails flapping in the wind. Sailors milled about, preparing the ship to set sail again.

Off on another adventure.

"I should go," Darian said, as Captain Carter waved at him, signalling that the ship was preparing to leave.

I blinked back the tears that burned at the corners of my eyes, giving Darian's hand a final squeeze.

"I'll be back," he promised.

We stood in silence, listening to the sound of the waves crashing against the shore. Darian leaned in, pressing his lips against mine. The kiss was sweet but it tasted like goodbye.

He pulled away, letting go of my hand, leaving it empty and cold.

I watched his retreating form as he walked towards the *Maryanne* and boarded the ship, blending in with the sailors who had been his family for years.

For now, his home and his heart was at sea.

I watched until the ship was a tiny white speck on the horizon. And I knew in my heart that Darian would keep his promise.

He would be back. One day.

Printed in the United States
by Baker & Taylor Publisher Services